BREAKNECK

BREAKNECK

a novel

by

Nelly Arcan

TRANSLATED by Jacob Homel

ANVIL PRESS / CANADA

Anvil Press Publishers Inc.
P.O. Box 3008, Main Post Office
Vancouver, B.C. V6B 3X5 canada
www.anvilpress.com

Library and Archives Canada Cataloguing in Publication

Arcan, Nelly, 1973-2009
[À ciel ouvert. English]
    Breakneck / Nelly Arcan ; translated by Jacob Homel.

Translation of: À ciel ouvert.
ISBN 978-1-77214-011-8 (pbk.)

    I. Homel, Jacob, 1987-, translator II. Title. III. Title: À ciel ouvert. English.

PS8551.R298A6213 2015   C843'.6   C2015-901432-8

Printed and bound in Canada
Cover design by Rayola Graphic Design
Interior by HeimatHouse

Represented in Canada by the Publishers Group Canada
Distributed by Raincoast Books

The author would like to thank the Canada Council for the Arts for its support in the
writing of this novel.

We acknowledge the financial support of the Government of Canada, through the
National Translation Program for Book Publishing for our translation activities.

The publisher gratefully acknowledges the financial assistance of the Canada Council for
the Arts, the Canada Book Fund, and the Province of British Columbia through the B.C.
Arts Council and the Book Publishing Tax Credit.

Their hands touched like twins, two delicate hands,
of the same kiln...

I

THE SKY AT HIGH TIDE

THIS STORY BEGAN under a summer sun, a year ago, on the roof of Julie O'Brien's building, where she was lying like an abrasion, a term she used to describe her relation to her skin, russet and fair, that came from Ireland if you followed it down from the third generation on her father's side, and that wasn't equipped, she told herself that day, to fight the burning sun that poured down and stung the nations of this world with its rays.

The roof of the building where she lived brought her closer to the sun and its needles. She imagined that day that this closeness was a match made to fail, that russet and blonde were lethal genes that couldn't survive the growing desertification of the world. She had another thought as well: that this world was a house and you had to be free to leave it if you wanted to stay.

The eight-storey building was full of people who didn't want anything to do with any of this, not because they lacked the heart, but because of what she'd thought about on the roof. The world was an oven opening onto hell, it was the assembly of billions of lives one on top of the other like a planetary neighbourhood, a harassment of opinions and demands, differences and denunciations, with its news reports and accounting of the dead, its pressure you had to avoid and its bedlam you had to flee, its incessant manifestations you had to repel if you wanted to live.

Julie had turned thirty-three that year, Christ's age as she liked to say, but that age was the only thing she'd shared with Christ. She had few friends who were growing ever more distant. There was that couple who just had a child, a little girl whose name she could never remember, a couple who used to be so hip and deliberately left downtown to build a life in the suburbs, choosing to send another soul to the stake, cast onto the global pyre. Her friend Josée left to live in New York for the opportunities it provided her career as an unemployed fashion model, and there she joined her New Yorker, a real Yankee who would give her American citizenship when they married—Josée whom she hadn't seen in years and certainly couldn't imagine having a child in New York, a roiling city of greenhouse gases, a city threatened by terrorism.

Julie was at the age when life pushed friends in different directions and children separated those who tried to stay close. This wasn't a problem for her, it wasn't even a shame, it was just the way things were and nothing more, she thought without irony when she thought about it at all.

It was noon and Julie had been tanning for an hour, burying herself deeper in her thoughts to endure the burn that, she hoped, would make her beautiful. In these days when success is the be-all and end-all, she told herself, slathering on a second helping of cream on her already burning skin, in these days when success shouts from every rooftop and age indicates the proper amount of success at every level, it's important to get your age out there. She never missed a chance to share her age: I'm thirty-two going on thirty-three, the age of Christ, I'm thirty-three going on thirty-four, she admitted with some chagrin, not wanting to let go of Christ. Julie gave out her age the way some people hand out their business card, it was the best way to solicit pity or stir envy, in her world where age was everything and nothing, a blessing or a death sentence, it was the most important thing of all.

She was of the age, she thought, when lacerations left by love had to be left in the past and when you had to think about children, to determine once and for all whether, yes or no, you could be a mother, and if, yes or no, the child would have a father. No, Julie wasn't a mother, and if by some misfortune—she told herself to instill both fear and reassurance—if one day she were to have a child, if one day her uterus found a way not to have its due ripped away in an abortion clinic, there would have to be a father to take care of it.

Thirty-three years old and she'd already written a number of documentaries, a few of which had been produced, and one of which had known a measure of success due in part to the title she'd given it: *Children for Adults Only*. The script featured the common yet undetected pedophilia of ordinary parents who can't let go of their children, who inspect them like a possession that can be turned inside out like a glove, children like handbags, with parents who make them live in a bell jar away from the world, to stave off bacteria and vexation, all for their own good, unable to leave them even for a moment. Julie trained the camera on parents who had become perverse through fear and precaution. They accused doctors, teachers, even the surveillance conducted by their cherished technologies of negligence, abuse, and violation of their children's right to remain intact through the vagaries of life. The documentary had a measure of success but didn't change social realities. Despite the convergence of the media when the movie was released, the documentary hadn't calmed the paranoia of pedophile parents and Julie didn't want a child just to put her principles into practice. When she considered that around the unstable nucleus of the world was an indefectible, unmovable aura, when she thought that beyond human mutation there was the homogeneity of cosmic law, inalienable, she was reassured, and she slept in peace. The world was hard-headed despite its upheavals; it never completely split apart, even if it went in every direction at once.

In any case, changing the world was not a concern of hers anymore at that point in her life, it hadn't interested her for some time, ever since she had lost her heart, or her soul if you prefer. She cared even less for the fate of her world that was bursting into flames all across the planet ever since she had killed the man who had wanted to give her a second chance and whom she believed she loved. That was Charles whom she would steal from Rose as a game at first, out of a desire to amuse herself, Charles whom she pushed into madness without much intention, Charles whom she killed without any motive—or hardly at all—almost an accident, through a plan unexpectedly fulfilled, and Julie almost guilty, with Rose as accessory.

This is what Julie retained from the event once it was over, since interpretations would differ. The rooftop was a starting point but there were others: for Rose Dubois, the starting point was found well before, and as for Charles Nadeau, he would never have the chance to tell the story of his own death. There are as many starting points in a story as characters in it, but the plurality of beginnings means nothing when the end result is the same. What counts, in truth, is the foundering, the location of its defeat, the moment when chance can no longer play a role, so strong are the movements that gave the story meaning that they hold it in thrall, pushing it toward its predestined end.

This beginning coincides with Rose entering Julie's life, or better still, her desire, she being the great helmsman of their fates, whom everyone had underestimated. Rose with her big ideas, who'd never been comfortable speaking, intelligence without language, without the means for language, beautiful beyond compare but never in her own eyes. Rose the fashion stylist who dressed her models with her own hands and needles in her mouth, who sometimes called the models bitches behind their backs on her off days because she could not actually slap them.

NEVER HAD THE sun seemed so close to the earth as on that day. The sun was frightening to behold, it looked as if it were kneeling and prostrating itself before Montreal's corpse like a moronic giant who doesn't know his own strength.

For the past few years, Julie had been tormented by the climate and temperatures that were no longer just conversation, but daily experience, worrisome over the long term because behind them hid a surge and a charge toward destruction.

One day she'd write a screenplay about what people had to say when nature stopped following the horizontal, solidly anchored mechanics of its slow evolution, when going against its own history, it unhooked itself from its heights and moved downward, broke away from its lofty distance and—you could never tell—one day it might dominate the lives of men and become the centre of all their concerns, like clemency or shipwreck, taking back the divine character it once knew and that men had stolen from it. It was important to say it out loud, Julie believed. Sitting among men and crushing them, nature would become God once again. Men would be forced to admit that their heavenly Father was not a father but an all-powerful child whose bawling blotted out the music of the world, keeping men from whiling away their lives in the idle comfort of their homes.

Her fair and russet skin, discreetly dappled, should be able to tan just like darker skin. But for that to work, she would have to accept that tanning wasn't an opportunity to bask in summer's touch, but a struggle, a duel between her and the world, a moment during which she had to concentrate and make freshness appear through her imagination, a number of minutes she'd have to suffer through, a time slot to let the burning spread without too much damage. The programmed desecration of russet skin, committed through strength of spirit, a fakir consumed by nails. In the heat of the day she had a thought for her microwave, then for her last lover Steve Grondin, the greatest pain of her life, the fatal one.

The smallest detail of that day, however insignificant, took on the proportions of a momentous event in her heart. Julie was on the roof, struggling to tan, when a song rose up around her, encircling the building with its incantations. It was a prayer of men calling upon Allah, Allah, Allah, a discordant word in her universe that knew only how to cultivate the body. These believers in Allah had in their voice their god whom they marched into the street, in a procession that threw them into a trance, and the song did not just go on its way, it didn't finish, it dragged on, as close as the sun. It was a beautiful song but that morning beauty exhausted Julie since it could not be present without the heat that coated everything, making it a burden. Today, at this very moment, she said to herself in burning revelation, beauty is a miscalculation.

From the roof Julie couldn't see the singing men because she insisted on searching for them among her neighbours, in the streets next to hers, neighbours whom she couldn't see either. To not identify the singers added another burden to her day, to the hobnailed sun that lowered upon her and began to correspond to God himself, nowhere, injurious, an ambush set at the edge of every horizon. None of her neighbours were visible, not even at the windows that, for the most part, showed only drawn curtains. The chanting continued to circulate without her or anyone else being involved, music with no other contribution than the voices themselves that at that moment seemed to be trying to be heard over eternity, an eternal sentence created by the obstinate belief of men in God, even in the Western world, where it existed the least, where we pretended to believe in nothing, only ourselves and the close reflection projected by the mirror of the present.

Just as Julie was about to give up and return to her place on the third floor of the building, she finally identified the place from which the chanting was coming, and who the men behind the song were. It was coming from the west, from Saint Lawrence Boulevard where she often walked, and it wasn't a Muslim chant at all, but the disciples of Krishna. From her roof she could see the boulevard as well as all the other Montreal landmarks: the Mountain bearing its cross, the Olympic Stadium, the Jacques Cartier and Champlain bridges, the major skyscrapers, not to mention the endless sea of roofs that constituted the real Montreal since they hid the daily life of its people, and its hidden heart ready to go out and beat in the streets, and make noise.

That the procession of singers were followers of Krishna and not Muslims reassured her, she didn't want the images of war seen on TV to take root in her indolent reality. The ridiculous nature of the Hare Krishnas made them innocent, their masquerade reduced their strength as a cult, they weren't about fervour but facetiae, not gravitas but indulgence. Hare Krishnas didn't march to carry on outstretched arms the coffins of their children who had been blown to pieces, but out of respect for the insects that might, who knows, be transporting the soul of their ancestors or be the future vehicle of themselves. People might gaze upon the Hare Krishnas but they didn't have to issue an opinion or make a judgement, they could laugh using the wide spectrum of laughter, from thigh-slapping guffaws to laughter that offended and destroyed.

JULIE WAS WATCHING the procession when Rose arrived. Like Julie she was wearing a bikini and carrying a pair of high-heeled shoes in one hand. Instead of lying down on a recliner, she came up to Julie, her free hand extended.

"My name is Rose. I moved into the building last week. Right across from your place."

Rose's story had begun months ago, unbeknownst to Julie. Rose had noticed Julie as her neighbour, Julie was someone for Rose, a threat, a blond-haired, light-skinned danger by her front door. The hand she offered Julie was slender, manicured, adorned with a ring, and the colour of her nail polish matched her bikini. Julie looked at Rose carefully because she was impressive. The woman was a true beauty, but in a commercial, industrial way, she noted that without judgment since she herself was part of that group of images and advertisements. Though she was only a few years past thirty, Rose, like Julie, had

had plastic surgery a number of times, and she recognized the signs, even the smallest ones, that indicated that something had disappeared, the impurities of old age had been erased from the surface of her body: an unmoving forehead, the flat contours of her eyes, without a single line even under the pressure of sunlight, the bridge of the nose bearing the nearly imperceptible mark of having been broken and remade straight and sharp, her lips swollen, rounded, half-open, like fruit on display. Her breasts were far more noticeable since they were a part of Rose that hadn't been erased, but filled instead, not oversized but with a firm roundness, implanted high on her body, giving the impression that they were an erect cock.

Seeing Rose was like pressing a finger against something inside her, the scar of her missing heart. Physically they looked like each other, but the likeness revealed another hidden woman, the way their lives were devoted to giving themselves what nature had refused. Rose and Julie were beautiful with a beauty that comes from privation, they assumed the right through contortions, their bodies sculpted by the gym, the sauna, the violence of surgery, an often irreversible roll of the dice, their nature torn asunder by medical technique and its ability to recast. They possessed the beauty that comes from the savage desire for the constructed self.

Then, Rose finally said, "I live with Charles Nadeau. I think you know him."

Rose looked at Julie, her eyes narrowed by the sun, though without wrinkles, and in return Rose felt herself weighed and measured and destabilized, undressed with that same attention to detail she used when she styled the models for fashion photographs. She was shorter than Julie but the shoes she dangled from her fingers had higher heels than Julie usually wore, as compensation for her size, a yearning to reach higher.

Julie couldn't remember a Charles but wished she did, since he was the reason Rose decided to establish her relationship, with a simple handshake, in front of her door.

"I'm sorry," she answered, "but I don't know Charles Nadeau."

Rose's blue eyes, no more than slits, showed her doubts. Out of embarrassment she looked off into the distance, toward Saint Lawrence Boulevard where the Hare Krishnas were still raising their song to the sky. Maybe Julie was lying to her, but that didn't matter, the die was cast.

"You've seen each other and talked in the neighbourhood. At the Nautilus. Often. He's tall and blond. A photographer. You also met Bertrand, a friend of ours, in the patio at Plan B. You told him you wanted to write a script on the world of fashion, and on Montreal photographers. It was one of your projects."

Rose had spoken her lines with the tone of a woman who'd been rehearsing them for a while, a reply casually dispensed with the quickness of words thought out ahead of time and repeated in front of a mirror, then kept close, waiting for the opportunity to have them heard by the party concerned. The line was both a demonstration and a warning, and each time Julie thought back to it, she was impressed by how it contained their entire story, how it held both prophecy and realization, a bottle thrown into the sea from high upon a roof, landing straight in the enemy woman's life.

It was true, not long before Julie had been approached in the street by a man, the same Bertrand she'd spoken to about a documentary project on Montreal fashion and its photographers, it was true he'd mentioned a well known photographer friend of his who was dating a fashion stylist.

Julie knew who he was, actually she had just discovered him. Watching Rose, she could picture him in quick succession in different parts of the city, at the gym and Java U, sometimes by himself, or with a woman who was out of focus, who must have been Rose, the impression of a woman gravitating around a man, Charles, whom she'd spoken to without remembering his name.

Every time they crossed paths he looked at her tenderly, it was a look that held her close but without the sexual aspect that so often hung heavily over the looks men who contemplated her body gave her, each time he seemed to look beyond her, to the background in which she was caught. She talked about weight-lifting with him and hypertrophic exercises, proteins and creatine, he wanted to invite her, in a moment of boldness, to have a drink somewhere nearby, in an outdoor café ideally, where you could still smoke, the patio at Plan B was a good choice. But before Rose stepped in, he was no different from all those who'd come before him, the others covered over by the boredom of a life without love, immersed in an indeterminate state created by years of anodyne encounters where faces and cocks blurred together, in an infinite number of combinations in a lottery nobody won. Charles, whose beauty she had never taken stock of, now took on the substance of reality, through Rose, he had become a semblance of a challenge, since Rose's goal had been to keep them apart.

After she'd finished her piece, Rose still looked at Julie, but her eyes fighting the sun no longer had anything to say, they simply showed regret. Julie felt that Rose had followed the path of her own thoughts as it so often happens to women who know by heart the truth of the things they fear, to such an extent that, despite their best intentions, they make it happen, simply by intervening in the way she'd just done. Perhaps Rose had understood her error and this forced her to continue on a different tone, with words that moved away from Charles, in an attempt to play down his importance.

"I hear there's never anyone on the roof. This is the second time I've been up here. The heat is unbearable."

A great silence came over them, a welcome truce for Julie, though painful for Rose. They stopped speaking to each other, looking at each other, they stood side by side, unmoving, Rose couldn't leave because she'd just gotten there and Julie was looking for the exit. Julie, voluble, the chatterbox, couldn't find anything to say as she felt an emotion suddenly rising inside her, almost imperceptible, a slight pinch that absorbed her attention since it was so rare. Charles had made an appearance in her mind and she began thinking of him, wondering where he might be now, maybe she would go with him for that drink at Plan B, scraps of emotion quickly dissolved in the heat that enveloped everything in his embrace, the sky like a sponge that had reached its limit, and now had to purge, perspiring, sweating profusely, beads of water running down its own walls. Clouds had formed and they began piling upon each other, capturing and snaring once and for all the life underneath, Montrealers thirsty for celebration. Just then a racket of honking exploded from Mount Royal Avenue, leaving just enough room to hear the cries of victory, happiness shouting and shrieking, without speeches, brute joy, an assault.

A number of cars had stopped at the light on Colonial Avenue, filled with men accompanied by their females, bellowing, from their windows they waved three-coloured Portuguese flags and something else inside, a scribble, an indefinable emblem from the rooftop. More cars filled with screaming and festooned with flags crawled in both directions on Mount Royal Avenue, going toward or having passed the Hare Krishna procession, the cars were so loud they would erase the Krishnas from the consciousness of Montreal.

A soccer game had just ended, and another one was beginning, the game that broadcast the good news through the city, not through the spirit of God but of Sport, good news launched into the streets as the Krishnas had attempted before them. The game would continue with its millions of fans, the clamour of the World Cup was beginning to resonate in all the big cities of the world. The Portuguese had defeated the English and Montreal's Portuguese, as well as fans of the Portuguese, for the rest of the day and through the night, lay endless siege to the city, criss-crossing its major streets, forcing their flags on the public as if it were the end of the world, and their right to drive through the streets in joy, and Montrealers would agree, admiring the courage of their national pride, their audacity in proclaiming their identity, they would see in them a warrior attitude they had lost long ago, the way your back straightened and you could stand tall, instead of eternally picking at your own conscience.

Julie could sense in herself the symptoms of that national self-examination, the common enterprise that consisted in self-flagellation, standing in the grandstands of the world, watching it like a stage on which other people lived, whereas her nation lapsed into boredom and torpor, flight, death by denigration, belittling, the weakening of fathers, the death of a soul that could strike a nation, leaving an entire people to reproduce inside their own tombs.

But that day Rose wasn't insipid, she didn't have that feeling of distance from others, on the contrary she was filled with a state of urgency and immediateness. Julie disoriented her, offered her no purchase, what's more she had eyes that Rose saw for the first time, unexpectedly of a rare green, emerald wonders that took her breath away. Meanwhile, Julie had identified the fear in Rose, she had felt it, weighed it, she knew she had gone further than she wanted to. Rose was exposed in the middle of a shooting range, everything was falling apart, yet she had to push on.

"Do you have a boyfriend?"

Rose opened a door for Julie, an opportunity, she was offering her hand so that she might be helped.

"Yes," Julie lied.

Julie was looking for a continuation, a name to offer that she couldn't find, a situation, a way to flesh out her lie.

"We're not living together yet, but we will. He's an architect."

The heat, the honking, the screaming, and Rose herself suddenly became intolerable, her existence was no more than armour against life, against the world and all it contained.

Rose watched Julie, she was smiling with her mouth but not her eyes, she didn't believe her.

"I hope it'll work out. Living together can really change a relationship."

That was all there was to say.

The sky changed colour. Without warning, it turned grey and dropped even lower toward the women, curving, seemingly moving toward its own centre. The sky folded over itself, an angry grey mass carrying as much water as a lake and which, helped by a strong wind that suddenly flared up, emptied itself upon Montreal like a giant letting go, clouds scattering across the sky as thunder and lightning finished them off. Something up there went beyond their understanding, a presence carried by its own gigantic motion that overcame everything in its unconcern, without a thought for the men it oppressed.

All this had taken no more than a few minutes to come together, to mobilize, to generate an extraordinary event, flamboyant, the climax of the day up there on the roof, that neither woman would forget, it would mark their lives by immortalizing their meeting. For Julie it would remain a symbol for the whole world, the power of mighty nature throwing back mankind's arrogance in its face, God as a churlish child. For Rose, it was a far more personal symbol, the entire world was communicating something to her, as a response to her mistake, forcing the sky over her head on Colonial Avenue to tell her something terrible, because of Julie, because of the meeting she initiated.

Lightning, the central part of the sky, had struck three metres from them, on the wooden guardrail against which they'd been leaning. They never heard such a sound, a detonation that carried the weight of a plane crash, they had never felt through their bodies such a powerful shock with such enduring weight, it lasted, obstinate, in the air around them, it filled the space like a lead wave. In the noise that forced their eyes to close, neither Julie nor Rose saw the splinters of wood exploding in every direction, but they felt the guardrail reeling under their hands. Rose had the clear sensation that her high-heeled shoes were thrown forward, down the emptiness of eight floors, as the number five hundred flashed in her mind, the price of the shoes she'd dropped and weren't hers, shoes she'd taken from some designer collection the day before. The shock pushed the women backward, synchronized, the two women in their bikinis swimming through the crashing rain as they cried out in unison, synchronized there as well, together and useless in the chaos, Rose fell to the ground, protecting herself in her fall with the hand that dropped the shoes, and Julie, once she found her legs, left the roof running, leaving Rose behind, alone in the storm, on the ground, next to the guardrail struck by lightning.

II

SHAPED IN THE SAME KILN

HER GIVEN NAME was bestowed on her by her mother, and her father's inattention, at least that's what she told herself. All her life she had tried to explain away her name, since everyone, except her mother and father, with a modicum of good taste and good sense could feel—despite the image of gentle fragrance it implied—that something was wrong, and that it came from the mother's side, a kind of abuse, worse than a spelling mistake.

She was called Rose and her mother Rosine, you can't imagine, she'd confide to people she met and whom she'd introduce herself to as a protestor against mothers and their choice of names, and husbands too.

Her mother had chosen the name to insert herself into her daughter, it was quite clear, and her father hadn't seen the Rose motif in Rosine's choice, and by letting her choose, her father had sacrificed his daughter by not paying attention.

Her mother had given birth to five girls and a boy: Lisa, Geneviève, Rose, Suzie, Marie-Claude, and Stéphane.

No sooner had she been born than Rose's personal drama began, she was stuck in the middle of a parade of girls and finally, as a reward and much to the Dubois family's great relief, a boy arrived who would become, against his will, his big sisters' doll. He was transformed into a possession that belonged to a plethora of little girls in little girl dresses bouncing up and down and clucking over him, and in the end, through sheer suffocation, lullabies and affections, they succeeded in breaking his gender, changing him into his inverse, a hole, a girl.

Rose grew up in a typical family unit in the town of Chicoutimi, in the Saguenay Lac-Saint-Jean area, in the midst of a swarm of females in a part of the country known for producing girls only. This proliferation of girls created her indefatigable perspective on the world. Even outside her native region, the surplus was obvious, everywhere she looked she saw the hateful distribution of the sexes that disadvantaged women who insisted on living and being part of the woodwork, so much so that she decided to dress them and make that her living, something that was also an abdication.

Julie revived that torment in Rose just as she was turning thirty, just as the question of affection and the love of men had found a solid answer in Charles, an answer she might have counted on for years to come. She told herself that Julie was only one woman among many and that it was a form of justice, for her and for others, she consoled herself by placing Julie in the logic of the overpopulation of women, those beings who required men and who weren't despicable individuals, of course, they weren't harmful in themselves, of course, but became so by the surplus they represented, and the war this surplus created.

Rose believed that women see nothing but what men want, they think of nothing outside of what men want. Women don't notice each other but for Rose it was the opposite, she saw them far too much, for her each woman should be questioned as to her motives, she was convinced that all women paid the price—it was clear, empirical, not subject to interpretation— for being more numerous than men. And a woman wasn't necessarily a woman. A woman was any being that gave its body to men, that wanted their body to meet men's, a man could be a woman in Rose's definition, as long as that man got hard-ons for other men. For her, gender wasn't defined by a person's genitals but by the genitals of other people, the one you dreamed of, and salivated over, to whom you gave a part of yourself if you were lucky. Not many understood this, and knew it to be true, Rose believed.

Her theories weren't politically correct. Theories are built on anomalies like homosexuality, she thought, and anomalies are often natural, she also believed, like homosexuality again. The anomaly when it came to women was that nature had decided they should be born in greater numbers in certain parts of the world, like in Saguenay Lac-Saint-Jean, to stockpile them in case of the extinction of the race, or massive loss of life due to an epidemic, without considering the happiness of those women without genetic or hormonal means to take up arms and establish an equilibrium. Very few women decided to fuck each other to find satisfaction because homosexuality was first and foremost a male thing. Easy to comprehend why, Rose believed, if you brought to mind the image of the hole you came out of.

Rose was a fashion stylist, she made up women for photographers, the clothes she chose for them didn't hide but revealed. She sculpted flesh for desire, for erections. The number of women grew with every picture, and in each one Rose left her mark, as small as it might be, in the sculpting of others, participating in her own disappearance. In her life she'd met women so beautiful she had to close her eyes from the shock. She named that moment of shock *the dagger*. A dagger to amputate her eyes, her heart, to suppress her own existence faced with dazzling light.

Many of the models were adorable, and Rose had appreciated a number of them for their kindness, their gentle souls, but more than anything she would look at them and each time be thrown into personal chaos.

Charles Nadeau was a photographer for whom she'd worked for years, and there was more tenderness in his eyes than his photographs. Pictures had to sell and selling was something that had to hit you square in the jaw, take you by the throat, at least that's what you heard everywhere that women became merchandise.

Charles the photographer didn't fall for models, against all odds he preferred Rose. Charles would remain for Rose a man who had fallen from heaven and given birth to her among the models, he had given her substance among the most beautiful of them, gradually beginning to notice her, over time, invisible in the pictures but always at his side, in the same studio, carting around the clothes and hanging them on racks, clothes chosen according to the desired degree of nudity.

Charles had loved her for years, Rose could never deny it, even after he'd left her. Her best memories were of the pictures that she was the centre of. Life is fabulous when it puts the lie to theory. Theories are built on disappointment, they aren't constructed to tell the truth but to force the truth to reveal itself and reject life, this she believed sometimes, when life was sweet, when a man had given her meaning.

Their story lasted five years. These days, Rose figured, that was a respectable length of time. Surely it would have gone on longer if not for Rose's mistake. Without meaning to, she had styled Julie the way she styled the models. She placed her in Charles' lens by making her move over to his side, his life, his work, and Julie let it happen the same way models let themselves be made-up, not out of vanity or cruelty, but boredom. Today Rose could say it: Julie was bored because her body had outlived the death of her soul, as Julie herself once told her. There was nothing in her body—a concept hard to understand if you've never died yourself—but her body remained sensitive to the life that existed outside it, and that life was a hard thing to tolerate. In emptiness movement no longer existed, or barely did at all: love and hate, basic feelings, had been replaced by the two monoliths of torpor and irritability.

ROSE WAS WITH CHARLES the first time they saw her, one afternoon at the Nautilus on the corner of Mount Royal and Saint Lawrence. The place practically empty, the air conditioning blowing hard enough to dry the skin off your bones, a lot of men for once, moving equipment that shifted more air than muscles, groans accompanied the lifting of weights, and Julie among the men with her body just muscled enough, developed with elegance, with her body that, for those who couldn't see past her façade, seemed filled with as much life as anyone else's; Julie looked like she had a soul.

At the Nautilus, Charles looked at Julie the way he looked at everyone else, one look, two, perhaps a third, because of his work as a photographer, he focused more, he was a master of composition too outside his studio, but also because Julie was the kind of woman he liked, medium height, curves rounded and full. But that wasn't all, she had more charm than most in the way she'd suddenly stop in the middle of her tracks to look out the window, her head in the clouds, far away, outside. But there were so many women in Montreal Charles found attractive, a fact that played against them. Maybe it even played against him as well, since he had slowly developed a resistance to his own tastes. Then Julie walked to him just like that, as if nothing in the world was simpler, maybe she had come looking for the weights he was holding and that she needed, the thirty-pound dumbbells. Could they share them? Okay for alternating, weights changing hands and hands touching out of simple necessity, an agreement that set Julie's attention on Charles whom she had never seen. Could he show her some exercises? Which muscles did they work?

Rose watched them with her stylist's eye, by reflex she observed Charles the photographer who so often came close to so many bodies. Patiently she held back, discreet, bent over her own weights that couldn't measure up to Julie's as with so many things, she would have the occasion to tell herself later. She left them for a time to their teamwork to concentrate on her own exercises, then she continued watching them, still at some distance, from a different angle.

Other meetings had occurred at the gym over the next few weeks, in the same manner, with first names exchanged and more glances in each other's direction, more words, verbal thrusts from Julie who had awakened entirely, though not entirely present for Charles.

These were mere details, but Rose the stylist noted them all. To be a stylist, she declared, was to see the details in women that separate them from the background, the absolute sex bombs, the ones who have character, the stars, and all the others while you're at it. Being a stylist means that when you walk down the street you look at every woman in isolation, to put her in focus for a photo.

The second time Rose saw Julie was in line at Meu Meu on Saint-Denis, still under an acid aggressive sun, filled with water, weighing upon the passersby adventurous enough to go outside, the weight lay upon everything that moved or slept with difficulty, like dogs. Julie was in front of them, a dazzling platinum blond, baby blond, defined shoulders above a thin waist, blue tank top and a jean skirt, looking over the list of ice cream flavours, or *gelato* flavours as Rose sometimes said to sound European. Charles watched Julie who was still to his taste, and did no more because he didn't know whether the shared weights and advice dispensed and the names exchanged were enough to say hello. Julie was looking at the large tubs of ice cream, and Charles watched Julie since she was still to his taste, but mostly to expedite the greeting, and fulfill his duty to be polite. He stared at the nape of her neck where a few errant strands of hair fell, waiting to greet her when Julie turned toward them, looking into each other's eyes, in torment, unsure of which flavour to go for or fighting the temptation of calories she wouldn't touch, then quickly leaving empty-handed without even greeting Charles or recognizing him. Rose wished that things could be left at that, but two other events took place, the least spectacular of which happened on the patio at Plan B.

The place was jammed with women and peppered with a few men, smokers most of them since a recently passed law prevented people from smoking inside public places, including bars. The sun, the crushing humidity, the sky ballooned with enormous clouds that barely let any air through, and only thick wet air, difficult to breathe, making you inhale with your mouth open like a dog lying in the shade, in the dirt. Rose checked out the women there and spotted Julie in the corner, she'd seen her at the Nautilus and in line at Meu Meu, she'd seen her dozens of times in the neighbourhood, and now she was sitting with Bertrand, her friend and Charles' too. Life is grotesque, she thought among them there in the outdoor café, sensing the dagger's approaching thrust.

Rose realized that Julie had always been alone when she'd seen her, everywhere she was alone, her friend Bertrand made her see Julie's solitude, though it was obvious, this was Bertrand she'd had in her bed before Charles, the man whom Charles pushed out of her life. Of all the men in Montreal, she told herself—even if there weren't that many—Bertrand would be the one to break her solitude, and make Julie a gregarious being like everyone else.

That day the couple was sitting in a way that kept Charles from seeing them, which gave Rose a respite, at least for a time. She would have to take the initiative, and stop the situation with her silence in hopes that nothing would happen, or force Julie's hand by way of an introduction, and maybe nothing would come of it. Bertrand sitting with Julie might bring Julie into Charles' vision by simple association; through Bertrand, Charles and Julie might find common ground, a place to meet.

Rose was about to force the meeting when Julie got up and took her hand bag, then shook Bertrand's hand and left without seeing them. A few minutes later Bertrand came up to them and sat at their table without mentioning Julie. Rose's torment, the dagger, the blade she used to amputate herself, kept pressing against her throat. She said nothing as the men spoke among themselves, leaving her outside the triangle. Concentrating on Charles' words as he regaled Bertrand with his upcoming collaboration with *Elle Québec* and another hypothetical shoot for a photo reportage in Africa. Vaguely following a conversation dampened by the heat concerning the space between fashion and human misery, forcing herself to remain ironic about the arrogance of imposing a stylist on AIDS victims in Africa for the hypothetical photos that Doctors without Borders was clamouring for. Rose realized in silence that she could not push Julie away from the outside, and in her desire to exorcise the dagger, she asked, "Who were you sitting with, just now?"

Rose's voice, caught in her throat, hobbled by her enemy, was so strange that Charles thought the question had come from another table. Bertrand opened his eyes wide, his two hands reached for his head in an indication of foolish forgetfulness and at the same time he brought Julie back to the patio at Plan B. Bertrand didn't answer Rose, but Charles.

"Julie O'Brien, the scriptwriter. Do you remember *Children for Adults Only*? The way parents reacted? Five or six years ago? They wanted it banned from the theatres. She's the one who wrote it."

Charles searched through his memory, barely functional in the heat and sun. He recalled something or other, but couldn't be sure because he hadn't seen many films in the past few years, and almost nothing from Quebec.

"I told her about you and your staff," Bertrand continued, motioning with his chin toward Rose. "She wants to write about fashion and photographers. With some sort of angle on nude bodies, or nudity as a disguise, how it hides women or something. The Julie O'Brien point of view is what I'm trying to say, hunting for vice."

Charles turned to Rose, trying to see whether Julie the scriptwriter was the same Julie from Nautilus, the same Julie who stood at the borders of their lives. Rose discovered that Julie was well known, she had written a movie that she'd liked, and she learned that Charles had been presented to her as a potential topic for a documentary in which she, Rose, Charles' excrescence, the shadow of his eye, the slave who organized, brightened, and showcased other women's beauty before exiting the frame where no one could see her, she, Rose, might have a role as a member of the staff. Then for the first time, Julie issued from Charles' lips.

"Blond, like very blond hair? Short? Green eyes? Like very, very green eyes?"

Bertrand's hands went up to chest level, and his hands made it known that Julie had much more than her eyes or her hair to make an impression.

"Yes," he added, dropping Julie's breasts that he'd mimed with his hands. "Single, talented, a bright future."

Four women stood up at the table next to them, making them move away from the hefted handbags and thighs climbing over them to pass. Among the women was Pauline, a makeup artist Rose knew from having worked with her early in her career as an intern. Rose didn't return her smile. She wasn't there for Pauline—the conversation between Charles and Bertrand that didn't concern her, where she didn't belong, pulled her in. Rose didn't know what ritual to perform to parry Julie's dagger, she didn't have the tools yet to neutralize this growing threat that occupied the entire sidewalk café, as large as the world, nailing

Rose to the spot, forcing her deeper into her nothingness, a threat that would not disappear or leave at the end of the day like a fashion model after a shoot. Charles leaned back in his chair, master of the conversation.

"I know her. I've talked to her a lot at the gym. She asks me for advice. We've talked about this and that but, strangely, never about work. How did you meet?"

Bertrand was already looking elsewhere, there was so much to see at the café that was as good as Julie, more beautiful than her, so many women that *beat her hands down*, he told himself, his mind filled with burning images.

"I went up to her in the street an hour ago and asked her to go for a drink," he replied, his eyes wandering to bare legs under the neighbouring table where two women sat. "The sort of thing that never works, usually."

"And she said yes, just like that?"

Charles was offended, as if his own past rejections should be compensated by Bertrand being rejected too. Bertrand reacted with a vague gesture, as if to refuse all credit.

"After I insisted, yes. I see her all the time in the neighbourhood. She looks cold from a distance. And she stays cold when she's sitting with you. And she doesn't drink, is what she told me."

Then Bertrand stopped talking for a moment to stifle a yawn.

"She used to drink, but now she only partakes of mineral water and grenadine. A real lady."

A long silence fell, like the end of a conversation. Bertrand glanced idly at his watch, Charles' head was in the clouds, Rose was waiting for the other shoe to drop, she felt it coming the way you smell a storm brewing. A child yelled from the other side of the cedar hedge that delineated the café as the sun hovered a few feet from their heads.

"Oh, I almost forgot!" he suddenly said, like a runner catching his second wind. "She left me her phone number. Thanks to you, Charles."

He placed a small piece of paper with Julie's number on it on the table, a bit of Julie set between them like a trophy or a gift. A tithe for Charles the photographer who could pick it up and place it in his pocket if he so desired, this small piece of paper marked with another woman that Bertrand finally picked up again, oh, thank you, God, Rose prayed, thank you for discarding the fragment of that bitch that Bertrand, thank God, slipped back into his shirt pocket, a flowery Hawaiian shirt, showing off. They went on discussing her coldness, what might be its origin, then the changes she'd undergone, referred to by Bertrand who'd been tracking her from a distance for years. Weight loss brought on by drugs, the way she had of avoiding eye contact, drinking too much by herself in the far corner of a bar, her reputation for being a slut, an impression of mental filth, an aura of foulness and ruin reflected in her eyes and skin, then a slow resurrection of her body, her blondness growing even blonder, her head held high showing signs of health, a firmer stature, anchored, a sense of propriety in public, the recovered dignity of a woman who'd gone bad. A woman killed by love, Rose would later learn, who had found a way to walk again, to breathe.

Something in the world collapsed for Rose that day in the patio at Plan B. The beginning of the end of her reign; soon new royalty would merge to take her place as she fell. Rose found herself in the uncomfortable posture of her own fall, shambling, dragging, out of Charles' life, a fall that would give her time enough to see what was coming, unhurried, but inevitable. Rose knew that without the need for distance, she knew it somewhere inside herself, as is sometimes said, her little finger, her antennae, her sixth sense, all to service her failure.

Two weeks after the events at Plan B, the couple's move struck her like an oracle's prophecy. Rose and Charles moved in right in front of Julie's door, in her building, on Colonial Avenue. You can't even begin to understand, Rose would complain to whoever might listen, once the damage is done, once the facts are established, you can't even begin to understand how life possesses me, toys with me, Rose in Rosine and then Rose in Julie, the neighbour across the way. Rose was absorbed a second time by a woman she didn't want and from whom she couldn't escape, except if she moved again, and immediately. Julie was closing in on her life, materially, inescapably, inexorably, as her neighbour. Rose could do nothing about it, she'd often explain her misfortune from the inside, through the substance that made her who she was, some gene pummelled into her by her mother that she now had to carry, that threw her to the wolves, strong enough to keep attracting new wolves to the door, a gene like a magnet that attracted defeat from afar, or pulled her out of her orbit into a crash course.

Rose didn't know right away that she had moved into Julie's building. The day that followed the move, she saw her walking down the hallway, wearing shorts and high heels, a manicured hand jingling her keys. Julie looked at Rose without seeing her. Her presence could only mean that she was after Charles, she was coming for him, Bertrand had called her and she'd then called Charles in a logical progression, to meet her subject, her way of writing. On the other hand, there was the fact that Charles wasn't there. He had gone to the studio for the day where he did his work.

It took Rose a while before she understood that Julie was living in the apartment across from hers, on the border of her home filled with cardboard boxes left unopened since work continued.

·But she had to leave. After she saw Julie in the hallway, she needed to go buy men's clothing since it was a male model, a popular singer, guitar-player, and songwriter Charles was shooting that day. Rose didn't dress men very well since she had never learned to study them. She had this theory that men weren't erection material for women, instead men's bodies were like magnifying glasses that they ran across women's skin to observe its grain, and then, and only then, came women's erections, under the gaze of that magnifying glass in which they contemplated themselves.

She only had a few hours left to find a buckskin jacket that would reveal the man's chest, jeans, leather boots, leather belts with a steel buckle, sunglasses, and bracelets, and cowboy hats that would shade the eyes and give the shoot the feeling of a duel. Downtown, there were any number of shops side by side where she was known, she could walk in searching for whatever new accessory might highlight the youth and coolness of a pop singer who played the guitar. Rose picked the clothes at random, organizing the colours with no regard to the usual rules of fashion, a lapse that was not like her. She didn't even take the time to chase after the parking ticket the wind had blown off her windshield, and on Saint Catherine West she ran a red light on her way to the studio and narrowly missed a pedestrian.

The shoot was scheduled for Charles' studio, but Rose stayed in the building where she'd seen Julie, trying to link her being there to an explanation she couldn't find. The singer she was supposed to work on made her think of Charles, whom she had to forget, and Charles whom she had to listen to but not look at made her think of Julie who, in her mind's eye, kept walking down the hallway of what should have been their sanctuary. She kept seeing Julie on a loop, emerging from the elevator and moving forward, always with a different outfit, like a fashion show, *haute couture* on high heels, jingling her keys like castanets from a manicured hand, poised, cold, regal.

The singer was kind to her but didn't particularly like the clothes she had picked out. Just because he played guitar didn't mean he had to dress like a cowboy. Just because he was popular and everyone liked him didn't mean he had to play the whore in this travesty. Despite everything, Rose came off not too badly, she figured, in the studio, protected, safe from Julie who might have been—who could tell, she worried—haunting the hallways of her building with her confident, cadenced, clicking gait.

Normally, photo shoots weren't danger zones. The models who paraded past Charles weren't the same as Julie. Their simpering airs were paid for and even if, in their world where they had to be picked out of a crowd, the keys to their advancement often lay with photographers. Charles resisted them, at least at this point in his career.

The hard part about dealing with models wasn't seeing Charles photograph them, but getting used to the suffocating feeling their beauty caused. Models were oppressive, unanimously and unilaterally, except when they grouped together and tallied up their complexes, when they banded together to attack the strongest, the most beautiful, comparing, and find themselves wanting.

Being a stylist meant finding a way not to feel bad about yourself when you faced the way other people were superior. Being a stylist meant working for their superior side, your job was to add beauty onto the foundations of their beauty that hurt you. Rose wasn't tall, and that made it impossible for her to even consider measuring up to them, since transcendence was nothing, and a magnanimous soul bullshit. Her small size summed up her role. With the models high on their heels, her eyes were on a level with their breasts, finely formed and girlish.

It hadn't always been so easy. One day Charles was late, and she started fitting clothes on a teenager to get a head start. The girl would go into the changing room and come out with a different outfit on her back. Rose watched as she forgot about the little room and undressed in front of Charles who had finally shown up, in the middle of the studio, refusing Rose's offer of a blanket that she held up like a makeshift screen. The girl took her clothes off and put on another outfit as Rose the stylist assisted her, forced to ignore the situation, retreating behind her body as she undressed at a slow pace that revealed everything, with the casualness of a woman who never missed an opportunity. Rose found a name for this sort of woman, this way of being, a name meant to hurt: bitch. Bitch to signify the split, moving from being a passive audience to a judge, answering with her own dagger and entering the battle. Bitch to keep her integrity in her distance from this foreign race. A race of young bitches, she liked to imagine, playing off the tension they created, dreaming of leaving the Montreal kennel to go and bitch in a larger universe of bitches, like Milan.

Models were categorized as bitches depending on their aggressive intentions. Through comments implying that Rose was out of place, by unneeded exhibitionism, by selfishness pushed to the limit that revealed unhappiness, disorder, the inability to digest, by a display of prideful prostitution, by a desire to crush, hurt, torture. Their bodies and features and words and work and slinking across the studio displayed their bitchiness, made them bitches, bitch a brutal word, a metronome giving the shoot its rhythm, bitch like a position to fight exclusion and obliteration, bitch for the pins to pin on clothes that were often too ample for skinny bodies, bitch for each tooth of the comb through each strand of hair, and every touch-up that Laurent, official hairdresser and makeup artist for the team, performed, each time a bit more powder on already perfect cheeks, bitch for poses held perfectly for hours, for the lighting and even for everything Charles did and said, since he too was sucked in by the bitchiness of the models despite his best intentions.

One truth saves us, Rose thought, us other women, a very simple truth, attested to by statistics: models aren't only beautiful to photographers but to all men, they can choose men in prestigious positions, in the movies, music, sports. One fact that played in her favour was Charles' lack of sexual attraction to models, which Rose had always only half-believed, since she couldn't explain it to herself, because Charles' absence of attraction seemed like a cover, a white lie about his secret desires, dangerous, that his denials kept hidden.

After the move there was Julie on the roof, the cursed roof on which a few other tenants sometimes tanned, the way white people bereft of colour tend to do.

It was possible that Rose made a mistake. That on the roof that day she only managed to rouse Julie, and create movement where before there had been only death. When you fear a woman, she told herself over and over again after the fact, it's best to remain calm. When you fear that a man might leave you, don't alert the neighbour women.

In her distress her theories sounded true. Montreal held even more women than usual. At Plan B, it was three women for one man, at the Baraka and the Assommoir, the ratio could be even more tilted. In Mile End and in the restaurants on the Plateau, it was a constant numerical disadvantage for the always too-numerous women who, to make matters worse, seemed younger with each passing day. Going to Montreal's hot spots demanded a fair measure of abnegation, Rose deplored. During this period she began feeling a new emotion, many-pronged, venomous, corrosive, a spell, an acid reaction handed down by her mother who, one day, couldn't deal with only having daughters and began rejecting them, starting with Rose, the third daughter, in Rose's case it had lasted almost a year, the longest duration of rejection among the siblings. This new emotion was a hatred for little girls, the baby girls who kept multiplying around her—at least so it seemed to her—and gathered around their mothers during summer strolls, hand in hand, one next to the other, in horrific combinations. Bunches of little girls in which you could see sisters, in whom the scourge of a lack of men was replicated. But this hatred she felt for the new generation of girls that would perpetuate the tension of their numerical asymmetry, the tension of competition between them, was nothing compared to the pity she had for herself. She was incapable of accommodating herself to reality, and granting herself the possibility of happiness since after all she was here, in this reality and not elsewhere, alive, small, but still young. Instead, she had to let the vise tighten around her, she had to press her own hands on the vise to tighten it further, she had to lend a helping hand to what was crushing her and contemplate, in Charles' life, her own destruction.

Julie on the roof was visible all the way from Mount Royal Avenue. Rose recognized her by her short hair, almost white. Her shoulders had become familiar, and tanning was the sort of thing she'd do, especially standing, looking toward the horizon. Rose had first seen her from behind, a fine muscular build weakened by the sun, bent over the wooden rail that kept her from falling. They were both wearing bikinis like true Montreal women, always expecting to be photographed, always ready for the perfect shot. Even from behind, Rose could tell that Julie was deep in thought, she was in dialogue with the world before her, conversing with her words, always sylphlike, words that surprised, opinions that shocked, that Charles listened to, her beliefs elaborated into sentences woven around the thoughts she expressed. Julie was a woman of the mind, even if she worked hard on her muscles. And her muscles, Rose hoped, were a way of thickening the wall that separated her from her emptiness.

As she came closer, Rose hesitated, maybe because of the sun's glare, she thought. Could Julie not hear her because of the heat? But it was too late, she was already standing next to her, with her reasons for being there.

"My name is Rose. I moved in across from you a week ago."

Their hands touched like twins, two delicate hands, of the same kiln, Rose thought, despite Julie's superior height. Julie hadn't spoken her name, she might have been saving it for a special occasion. From up close, Julie's eyes took her breath away. Their beauty came from neither makeup nor the hands of a surgeon. Her eyes betrayed her thoughts, a farandole of words, her eyes picked up signs wherever they lingered, they searched you for information, to read you. Julie looked Rose over from head to toe, top to bottom, discovered the traces left by rhinoplasty on her face, noticed the tone of her nail polish and the colour of the shoes she held in her hands, shoes that cost a fortune but that she hadn't paid for. Julie devoured Rose the way Rose devoured other people, Charles' women chopped into particles then rebuilt as a single unit in a photo. Rose felt her eyes on her like an understanding of what she was, of a beauty similar to hers but also her being as a whole, in this moment where they searched for sisterhood. This woman had once been capable of love, Rose—who'd heard Julie's story through Bertrand—said to herself, and her eyes revealed that truth, they sought a way back to love. Time to push forward, she told herself, and turn her away from my door.

"I live with Charles."

A slight change in the shade of Julie's green eyes, turning away from Rose.

"I don't know any Charles."

"You talked to him at the gym. You asked him for advice. A photographer. Bertrand from Plan B talked about him too. You told him you were looking for a photographer for a documentary you're writing."

Julie's eyes floated back into thought: she remembered. Rose had said too much, or maybe not. Julie's door faced hers, which would have brought Charles to her eventually, or Bertrand would have given her his phone number. In any case she was surrounded.

The truth was that the three of them crossed each other's paths in the neighbourhood, everywhere but in the building's hallway. For weeks Rose had counted Charles' steps as he moved toward the elevator, her ear against her front door, and each time he left home by himself. His steps never hesitated. A few times she heard his voice on the phone, other times the ringing of the phone itself, an irritating music, an interruption from the outside world in synthetic blues. But she never heard him speak with Julie. Neighbours, she wrongly concluded, instinctively know how to keep the peace. Neighbours don't really like having neighbours, but they get used to them by getting to know their private noises, the comings and goings of life in a residential building.

On the roof, nothing had moved between the two women. There was a silence during which Rose attempted to see what Julie was looking at in the distance, a world of activity outside that didn't interest her but captured Julie's attention: the racket of the soccer fans celebrating a victory by honking their horns, cars seen from above, filled with fans, a sky preparing for battle, turning grey. Rose couldn't look at any of that for any length of time, she was too busy trying to find something to say, that might give her reason to celebrate, to save what she thought was lost.

"Do you have a boyfriend?"

"Yes. We don't see each other very much but we want to live together. He's an architect."

It might have been true but Rose had her doubts, her sixth sense told her. Because of the architect business, a profession that seemed pulled out of thin air. Because of Bertrand, who never noticed an architect hanging around.

"Well, I wish you the best of luck," Rose continued, suddenly feeling the dagger's thrust, a shallow drag of the knife without warning, like an impulse.

"Moving in together can be a test for a couple."

Again, the silence between them; Julie tired of being there and Rose ill at ease standing next to her, claiming some kind of right over Charles. Then, in defiance of her will to act and construct her happiness, a downpour swept them away, followed by lightning that had destroyed the wooden guardrail next to them, a horror of noise and power fallen from the sky, an obstacle in her path. This was what the storm was telling her: understand that there was nothing to gain by resisting, it wasn't only the multitude of other women who could take Charles away from her, but the world as a whole, its devastating power that watched her and followed her every step. Her shoes fell from the building. At the same time the number 500 struck her like the symbol of her loss, just before she fell to the ground, injuring her wrist.

Rose watched Julie run to the staircase that led inside the building, then stayed on the roof a moment, buffeted every which way by rain so dense she couldn't see a thing, so opaque that the bottom and the top, the behind and the before, lost their place. She wanted to stay on the roof to cleanse herself of herself, and end it all right then, halt what had not yet happened. A power had pushed her out of her project, prevented all sisterhood and brought her back in line.

At the foot of the broken railing, Rose didn't even have the dagger anymore to keep her company. From that day on, she knew, her days would be a desertion, from that day on, she would be nothing.

III

THE TROUBLE WITH BEGINNINGS

JULIE O'BRIEN WAS AT home on Colonial Avenue, lying prone on her leather couch, eyes on the ceiling, thinking of Steve Grondin, her last lover. In four years she'd seen him only six times, six times her soul re-entered her body like a warm mouthful, a swallow of smooth liquid, smooth poison, she was thinking as she lay on her back that there was always something unpleasant about meeting him, a warm unpleasantness emptied her. Six times she suffered from weakness that began in her chest like lava, flowed into her legs that suddenly went feeble, a pair of rags. She would lose her sense of direction when she saw him, sometimes she acted like she was talking on her cell phone with someone. Each time, for days, she kept the image of Steve seen furtively, walking on the other side of the street, or his elbow on the bar, always surrounded by women, never the same ones, with no idea she was there, most likely concentrating on what he shouldn't be doing, preoccupied with ignoring her, not giving her the slightest sign, indifferent, having seen her but forgetting her immediately. Indifference was a state that tormented her because she couldn't be indifferent due to her emptiness that left her feeling alone, the shock of seeing him from the outside, the feeling of neither warmth nor chill that was the opposite of who she was, the absence of a reaction that hurt her, and reduced her to nothingness, unworthy even of contempt. Other people's indifference always forced you to react, she concluded when she thought of him. Faced with nothing, you had to deal with hard emotions—you were forced to feel.

Meeting him six times over four years was something on the Plateau where everyone was always bumping into everyone else. Lying on her brown couch, she understood why she met him so rarely: Steve had a car. She was surprised she never considered that possibility, since she'd visualized the routes he might have taken so many times. It was clear, Steve had a car because he was rising through the ranks in his profession—and why wouldn't he be?—driving a Mini Cooper, accumulating success, just as she had hoped for herself. Steve had become successful in a craft she'd never master. He was an editor for movies, reportages, and documentaries, a profession that would forever keep him from public recognition and celebrity. Julie was happy he wasn't a public figure like some of her exes. Happy she wouldn't bump into him each time she opened the newspaper, happy he didn't exist in the mass media to which he contributed. But once the car had been established, the possibility that he had changed professions also became something to consider, maybe now that his job was in the public eye, he could be married, the father of a child—and why not?—a rising father driving a Mini Cooper, a wife by his side.

The possible promotion of her lovers, their change and progress, troubled Julie so much she used to drink, vodka and white wine, to calm her upheaval. She drank to prevent this compulsion that made her create a life for him through endless scenarios, and to stop the pain of imagining him—even if it was only in a dream—continuing his life without her. Essentially, she drank to check the constant storytelling of what had become his life and, just as she fell into unconsciousness, stop it entirely. She had fallen into unconsciousness more than a hundred times over the past few years, more often than not at home, but sometimes on the ground, in parks, alleyways, or the building's hallway, and she suspected that the times she lost consciousness had led to the destruction of her soul. She brutalized her soul in her loss of consciousness, she disavowed her own being, so that nothing, not even shame, could bring her back.

She drank without ceasing for three years, then slowly started to quit, slowly started to forget, but when she got back on her feet she realized she was no longer capable of desire, be it for love or sex. Her pussy had rubbed against so many cocks over those three years, but now it no longer responded to anything, even her most perverse fantasies. That part between her legs that once demanded so much no longer wanted anything, and Julie felt nothing about this new state of being, nothing except perhaps a sort of relief at the death of her pussy that made all other deaths easier to take. The disappearance of her desire was followed by an extraordinary intolerance to movement, sound, to anyone else. She rejected all manifestations of the outside world: the weather, the phone ringing, traffic, road work in the neighbourhood, buildings being built, drivers and pedestrians, even her work as a scriptwriter, for which she no longer felt anything but weariness.

To bring a project to fruition, she needed far more time than before, and she took long and frequent breaks from lack of energy. Life had a listless heart that kept her from moving forward, advancing in her career, the normal progress. Only physical exercise retrieved her from the minimum state required to stay alive, the smallest effort of daily life, she liked the pain that didn't disfigure her the way alcohol had, and appreciated the results. She managed to achieve the rare feat among white people: she had a black ass.

With the years Steve had faded and lost his substance. He was still present, but difficult to grasp, he slipped between her fingers not because he refused her embrace, but because she had no more strength to embrace him. Often she would bring him to the forefront of memory but never for extended periods of time, and with no great emotion. Lying on her couch she tried to imagine his car but immediately lost interest, Mini Cooper or not. No sooner had he taken shape than she drew away, into the distance of four years of absence, four years without a word exchanged, without a sign.

Then Charles Nadeau came and replaced him in her thoughts as she examined the grey cement ceiling of her apartment. For the past month Charles had made his way into her, like the beginning of a love story. A man lived in her, him and his cock would soon push themselves inside her and mould her to their shape.

She and Charles had crossed paths in front of the building a few days before, they agreed to have a drink and chat about the documentary project Charles knew about. She wanted to talk to him about her approach that was far from journalistic, her intimate way of seeing the subjects she treated.

The crowd was thin on the Plan B patio, the heat bearable, the sun dry, high in the sky. Children played behind the cedar hedge, their presence like a reminder to the customers not to go too far, like so many little judges reminding Julie of her past degeneration, when more than once she ended up on her back in the same playground when she left to go home after drinking too much, only to be forced out of her coma by the police, called by the neighbours.

She was grateful to the world for not oppressing her at this particular moment. She had to be in her best state of mind, alert and attentive to Charles. She was grateful too that the world let her present an affable face that gave her a chance of pleasing a man who liked her. She was feeling good even if alcohol threw its shadow over her, with its threat of a breakdown. She had to start somewhere; a tirade broke the ice.

"I don't study themes, but people," she began. Unconsciously, one of her hands grasped the bicep she was impudently flexing, a demonstration.

"Themes emanate from people. They shouldn't be forced to exist. They should come from people and not be the starting point. And I never know when I begin a project what I want to talk about. Which means that if I'm talking about the fashion world I might drift toward another topic with no apparent connection. The results are always very baroque."

Charles was staring at Julie's bicep as she solicited it with her hand, as if to measure its strength, attracting the attention of a few women around them, mineral-water prattlers. Charles didn't understand anything about themes that emanated from people or the baroque character or the results of the process. Baroque meant nothing except, maybe, objects and flaws. Baroque like gargoyles, demons, monsters, oddities and bad-taste baroque like gothic, adolescents wearing black over white skin, weighty and dramatic, haunting the Plateau Mont-Royal.

"Baroque?"

"Yes, baroque."

Charles was waiting for details that didn't come. His attention had moved to Julie's breasts that were filling him with a pressing desire to touch them. Nothing of what he heard pleased him but something in Julie's body, her firmness no doubt, attracted him. He wanted to possess, to make her his, and for that he couldn't get flustered and lose his edge.

"I've been a photographer for six years," he declared by way of an answer, folding his hands over his knees, an interview posture.

"Before, I was an assistant. I liked it, but it was hard at first. Montreal isn't very big, and there are a lot of photographers. Most models go elsewhere to get paid more. I work for *Elle Québec*, *Loulou*, *Summum*, rarely for *Vogue* or *Vanity Fair*. I shoot for fashion magazines, but I do events too…and overseas contracts…"

Charles continued dealing out information about himself, scattered every which way, slowly realizing he had very little to say. He was sorry, all the more so because he was having difficulty not dropping his eyes to Julie's breasts. But she was barely listening to him, knowing she would break down and drink, and knowing as well that to be interesting, Charles would first need to make a list of things that wouldn't be useful for them. She wished they could skip this fastidious part of character.

"Do you like your loft?" she asked to stop his prattling. "What do you see from your window? I'll bet it's the brick wall on the other side, right?"

As she spoke she watched the pack of cigarettes that peeked out of Charles' shirt pocket, feeling in the pit of her stomach the twinge that always preceded the times she drank, the malaise before the dissolution, the resistance of her body before the joy of falling apart. In a single quick movement she grabbed the pack, opened it, and pulled out a cigarette before looking up at Charles, waiting for him to offer a light.

"I'm not sure yet, it's pretty busy."

Concentrating on her cigarette, the first in six months, Julie hadn't heard him.

"What? Not sure about what?"

"The loft."

"Yes, of course, sorry."

"And there isn't a brick wall in front of my window. There's nothing special out the window, actually."

"You lived with Rose before you moved here? How long have you been together?"

"Four or five years, something like that. We didn't live together before, only next to each other, practically on the same street. In Little Italy."

"It's not bad there. Calmer. There's so much noise here."

Then, as silence fell, Julie noticed the desire in Charles' eyes for the first time, a desire like a light he shone on her, then a child behind the cedar hedge screamed in surprise and began to bawl with that end-of-the-world intensity Julie hated so much. For her, intensity was a serious mistake, inconsiderate when you considered other people's existence, and besides, the end of the world should be welcomed with the feeling of a mission accomplished, and not revolt and resistance.

"We should drink a little before we talk," she suggested through a mouthful of cigarette smoke.

"Anyway, my work and my life aren't exactly exhilarating," Charles admitted, unhappy at being so uninspired, and feeling he wasn't a very interesting subject.

Julie was expecting just that sort of reply; she wasn't of his opinion.

"Exhilarating doesn't interest me. I work with unease and guilt."

Charles disliked both unease and guilt. They didn't become him, and he couldn't understand how they could constitute a starting point for a project.

"We should have a bottle of white wine," she decided. "It's time for an aperitif. Do you like wine? Unless you want sangria?"

In the hours that followed, they drank three bottles of chardonnay. After a few glasses, it all disappeared, the documentary project, fashion, photo shoots. They relaxed and Julie was able to get what she wanted from Charles in little bits and pieces, and in the drunkenness that filled her, she began to listen to him, alcohol excited and lulled her at the same time, soon she entered that phase of general reconciliation in which every person with whom she'd ever crossed paths in her life was absolved, washed of all sins, when the greatest moments of disaster and the deepest depths of abjection took on a personal meaning bigger than her and that she had to accept.

Emboldened by Julie's body leaning toward him, encouraged by the questions she asked, Charles ended up giving in and talking about the butcher shop that Pierre Nadeau—his father—had owned, providing details he had promised himself never to express out of fear of unearthing everything, bringing to the present abominations best left in the past. The hesitation and distance that characterized him earlier suddenly gave way to uncontrollable outpouring. His fear of the taboo was suspended as his story took shape and as Julie, who didn't hear the children behind the hedge anymore, perceiving nothing but the extraordinary quality of his story, let her stupefaction show.

Of his childhood Charles retained only terrible and anxiety-ridden memories of large pieces of hanging flesh, his father's and his animals', a small room inside the shop filled with cold and the smell of death where his father would lock him in each time he had panic attacks and demanded to see his mother and sister who'd left to live in another city when he was twelve. He told Julie about his vision of pieces of meat splayed, dismembered, stacked together, the feeling that the essence of his life would stick to this flesh, and that he too would be cut into pieces and hung and, who knows, forced to forever remember this life where he and the carcasses formed a single body.

His sister Marie-Claude followed his mother Diane out of the city and he, Charles, had been forced to stay with his father in the house with its adjoining shop. It was better that way, his mother thought, to develop his identity, and grow up with the right gender, officially given at birth.

Pierre Nadeau not only had the brutal manners of a butcher, but a few defects in his soul he could blame on his own father, cracks through which insanity entered, real insanity, the kind that produces chattering voices that open onto invisible planes populated by beasts. Charles had a lot to say about his father who'd nearly driven him crazy: his explosive nature that erupted after Diane and Marie-Claude's departure, his state growing worse and more intense, which led to the loss of his butcher shop after a few years, before he ended up in the psychiatric hospital where he was to this day. His attacks, his descents toward hell, the uncontrolled slide had disturbed Charles and forced him into his father's darkness, where he witnessed his world in nightmarish snippets: the telepathy, the deathly dangers, murderous and mutant female assassins, informers from beyond the grave, signs of planetary catastrophes, conspiracies against him fomented in high places, within the Government, in the spheres of Supreme Power.

The sheer size and strength of Pierre Nadeau let him rule over the house, his son who was his only audience, where his insanity was law. Many afternoons, when Charles came back from high school, he had to help his father close up the shop, wrap pieces of meat, label them, and sometimes lug the large sides of meat that had been delivered by truck into the shop. Once the chores were done, father and son began the night's routine, at the end of which the son, more often than not, would finish his day in the cold room. The routine was a kind of ceremony. Charles wasn't hungry enough to eat the dishes prepared by his father. He would have given anything to finish off the plate of meat and potatoes but he couldn't, the meat was too close to him, from the family shop, meat made of the same bloody matter as he was, as red and painful as his own body, and the more upset his father became, the less Charles could face his plate, his father's elliptical speeches, his leaps of logic between subjects that had no link to what was in their plates, the treachery of women, the Amazons who had an eye above their pussies, or so said the father as he raged through the house with no regard for his son. He, the father, whom all wanted to hurt, needed to protect himself from the Amazons, sworn enemies of men, protect himself from them but also everyone and everything else, the G-Men especially, in cahoots with the Amazons and their superhuman sight, the third eye in their pussies that saw everything coming, especially him.

The father combined the most fantastic elements, thinking he could find truth in his constructed system, and understand better than anyone the planetary threats against humanity. He lost himself in his stories instead. Every time, Charles would moan and cry, unable to stay in one place, unable to feel comfortable anywhere, not even in his room from which he could hear his father's carrying on. Then his father reacted, finally Charles existed, he had to push his son aside, his existence was howling too loudly. He dragged him to the cold room, an old walk-in refrigerator that couldn't be opened from the inside. His son disappeared into it, partly so he wouldn't need to suffer his presence in his unfolding insanity, partly to protect him from it, for at times, when light broke through, he would see Charles' anxiety as he witnessed the insanity he wanted to cure. Almost always he would go and release him an hour later, two at most, but sometimes he'd forget him entirely and wake up in the middle of the night, remembering he'd forgotten. He would run to the cold room, sorry, sorry, and pull his shivering son out, still moaning, and envelope him in his rough tenderness, hugging him too hard, crying over him, choking him, sorry, sorry, tenderness that was, for Charles, worse than the hours of detention.

During his isolation in the cold and dark of the cold room, another war began, the one he had to fight, not against his father but against the thoughts that tumbled through his mind. The slabs of meat he couldn't see appeared in photographic detail, they were a presence in the room. Then there were noises, the kind that a footstep in a puddle makes. He heard the sounds of moving viscosity that reached for him in mortal embrace. Charles would try and disappear and breathe as little as possible, to escape the attentions of the butchery.

This nightmare lasted more than a year, then Diane took him

back and brought him to live with her and his sister in Magog, not far from Montreal. If his mother had made her move even a month later, it would have been too late, Charles believed, he would have gone mad, he would have fallen in with his father and his beliefs, his Amazons and global treachery. He would have done that out of a desire to survive, the way the spirit adapts to what's intolerable, faced with the shattering of expectations, the days of ruin with their infernal logic to which only his father held the key.

Charles couldn't stop talking, and as he told his story to Julie, she asked questions and offered opinions, she served him up a small masterpiece of interpretation: she told him why he'd become a photographer and why he didn't desire his models, why he loved the smooth unity of women's bodies in photographs, their integrity guaranteed by the images themselves, the glossy paper that turned their bodies hermetic, inalterable, without odour and by the same process without sexual energy, sublime but neutered. All that, Julie continued, because his father was a butcher. That explanation could have been perceived as a ghastly shortcut but it captivated Charles who was reliving his childhood with this woman he barely knew as his guide, she was revealing the essence of his life like a fortune teller, with two draws of her cards, the butcher who splays open, the photographer who seals tight.

By the third bottle of Chardonnay, Charles' story began to wither, it took a comic turn as Julie, still rehashing her theories about his career as a photographer, compulsively touching his shoulder, feeling her need for a man, a powerful appetite that hardened her nipples, a sign of health. Every five minutes they clinked their glasses together, cheers, to your health, making jokes about the World Cup fans they called "Free Radicals."

They were breaking open a fourth bottle of Chardonnay when Rose appeared, when they finally noticed she was standing next to them, unmoving, pale, almost blending into the row of cedars behind her, the same colour as her safari dress. She was stand-ing bolt upright by their table, looking at neither one nor the other but at a hazy spot somewhere between them, the two of them who'd forgotten her, Charles more than Julie. She looked like a statue but for the uncontained distress of her features, and she forced the reality of the outside world onto Julie, like an acci-dent between her life lived in a vacuum and the great obstacle of other existences, those other people who loved with all their hearts and imposed their suffering on her like a return to her past. Rose had been on the patio for the last hour, they'd later learn, watching them from the next table, drinking the same Chardonnay, as if to be part of them.

She'd heard the last hour of Charles' confession as he slowly drew closer to Julie, touching her elbow as she held onto his shoulder. Rose's world fell apart a second time on this same patio as she realized that Charles never broached the subject with her, despite the many attempts to learn more about his father. He'd never spoken of the cold room, he always claimed Pierre's insanity had been caused by depression due to overwork. He even alleged they'd gotten along well, and that he was sorry he had to go live with Diane and Marie-Claude.

"Hey! Rose! How are you?"

Julie was aware of the embarrassment of the situation, but she was having too good a time to give into it. She raised her arm in an attempted wave.

"I've got the same dress," she yelled, "only beige! Come and sit down!"

As she scanned the patio for a chair, Julie noticed that people were looking at her with that superior air in which she saw herself debased; she had felt that look before.

Still standing, unmoving, Rose could neither return Julie's wave nor leave. She had never felt so bad in her life, she was being forgotten by people and made to forget herself. She didn't care about keeping up appearances, so sharp was the dagger at her throat. On that day, as she was being harried from the world where the world itself was an image both crude and distant, she felt for the first time how close love could be to hate.

Charles was ashamed of Rose's intrusion, it forced him to confront another shame, worse than the first, of having dug so deeply into his past, into what was least respectable, under Julie's spell, her magnetism had made him reckless, more so than the wine, even though he wasn't used to drinking, at least not in such quantities and so early in the day. He got up, dizzy and upset, to take leave of Julie, kissing her on both cheeks, peck-peck, avoiding the subject of the full bottle he was leaving with her, and making no allusions to a future meeting.

Julie was drunk. She was beginning to dissolve. Her happiness had crumbled. It was too early to go to bed, too late to stop. She went home with the bottle of Chardonnay, got a glass of water, and swallowed two Xanax in front of the television set to make sure she wouldn't drink any further. Her body would be swallowed by a sleep that would prevent any more damage, sleep would accomplish what she couldn't do: she would stop drinking. She woke up eight hours later on the couch, in the middle of the night, in front of the snowy TV screen, the memory of leaving Plan B completely gone. As she stood in the warm water of the shower, at least she knew she hadn't done anything stupid. She hated her cowardice that always left her on the edge of some great fall, it pushed her into nothingness that wouldn't spit her out until it took a bite out of her, keeping a piece for itself. As she always did, she put an X on her calendar for the date of her relapse, the first in six months, and cleansed herself the following days at the gym, sweating, more than necessary, in the sauna.

IT WAS STILL EARLY. The sun was beginning to rise over the eastern edge of the city, sending its rust-coloured rays through Julie's window. Not that bad after all, she told herself that morning, recalling her relapse, she'd seen worse. As she lay on her couch, she thought of Charles, whom she believed she loved. She remembered his look on the patio that had lost the indifference of their first meeting, a look that took each part of her in, piece by piece. Alcohol had kept her from feeling the effects but now, on the couch, she felt them returning, the heat, the filling of her being that hardened her nipples, flowed into her pussy suddenly alive again, like a corpse rising from the grave.

She was afraid her emotions wouldn't last. Other men caused the same reaction over the years and none had lasted. Men encountered her hardness, her coldness, her frigid reactions to their attempts to get close to her that appeared early on, after a few days together, at most a week or two. Life had a special way of rigging every game, and she had her own tendency to get out of sync, the way she had of never having the right emotion for the situation. Never had Julie felt so loved by men as when she could no longer return their love.

Her family, those close to her, her colleagues, and even André the Giant Casanova, her only friend who never spoke to her in the language of love, claimed that her fear of being abandoned as she abandoned herself kept her from loving them. At one time or another, everyone had served her up the fashion magazine psychology about how people who loved no one were simply more sensitive than others, Homeric lovers changed into stone by adversity, people with hearts so great they became parsimonious with their affections. People are making things up when they think fear keeps me from loving, Julie said to herself, the fear of abandonment as if I could give a shit about their abandonment, everyone is in love with the idea but actually it's a material incapacity; my circuits are fried, the very flesh in which love takes root has been damaged.

Wounded flesh hides to heal. Julie lived in a downy décor, flowery, a cocoon that always embarrassed men who dared enter, so comfy everything was, all cushions and comforters, so subdued was her environment, filled with green plants where three Siamese cats slept at all times, the atmosphere discouraged movement. The setting was designed to reflect and contemplate on the past, a retreat against the grain of the world, its impetus towards efficiency and results. In Julie's loft there was very little effort, few results, but many rewards, those you enjoy sitting or lying down. She lived in a single large room where she could keep an eye on the pots on the range, lying on the bed, and her immobility, sometimes troubled by her cats that always moved in a pack, as by groupthink, was visible everywhere, in radius of three to ten metres.

The bathroom was immense, as big as the bedroom, which wasn't a room but a loft space that two chests of drawers, a lamp, a few plants, a desk and the brown leather couch circumscribed.

The bathtub was deep and wide, it faced a white tile wall on which large moving glass panes let Julie watch television while her body was immersed in bubbles.

Two days after the events at Plan B, she and Charles bumped into each other on Mount Royal Avenue. Charles smiled when he saw her as they moved toward each other on the same side of the street. He smiled as if she'd always been part of his life, as if he'd been expecting her at this very moment, as he was walking out of a supermarket. The way he was smiling wiped away the shame of his confession, as well as any shame at having been caught by Rose. They stopped walking to talk, both affected by that reserve that follows great declarations and epic gestures. They talked about how they might see each other in the future without being disturbed. The bar called Les Folies, not far from Plan B, seemed ideal since neither of them had ever been there, and since Rose would look for them in places they knew and patronized, like the Assommoir, the Baraka, and Bily Kun.

Julie had a sort of intellectual compassion for Rose. She knew she'd been for Steve the way Rose was now, a bitch sniffing for a trail, fearing recognition, a self-absorbed being you had to spare and get used to. Like Rose, she had seen another woman's filth demolish her life. She believed those stories are destined to repeat themselves, travelling from one existence to another, and that each woman was, by her nature, another woman's bitch. She wanted to enjoy being the strongest—especially since she'd suffered from being crushed before—to feel the ongoing triumph of her victory close to her heart, hold that happiness up and compare its longevity with the sadness that held her every morning when she woke. But of course suffering was in league with time, there was nothing fleeting about it, it was the backdrop on which fleeting pleasure was exhibited like a fit of the giggles, lightning, and fireflies.

On her bed, Chafouin, one of her cats, lifted a somnolent lid over his blue eye and moved a few steps to the left before stretching and lying back down in his own purring, identical to what he was. He settled in the same position through a seemingly useless effort, but which was necessary for him to renew his happiness at falling asleep, feeling night cover over his conscience again, a downy sleep in which downy dreams were dreamed, without conflict. Often Julie wondered if her cats had noticed the changes she'd undergone in the past few years, if they understood she had copied their way of being, a series of curled up positions, sleepy batting of her eyes not truly knowing desire, content to simply be, to prepare the ground to welcome her. Sometimes her newfound downy nature began to sicken her, and exert the same pressure the outside world did. Her immobility would fill with hostility and threats, insults shouted at her in the name of life that was happening someplace else, without her. Comfort began awakening a need to leave that same comfort, and the pleasure principle of letting go would become dangerous ground, a Pandora's box. In those moments, she would remember why she was dead. She was dead from an excess of will, perseverance becoming all, she was dead in her determination as life commanded her to give up, and withdraw herself from the world. She was dead from her refusal to suck it up.

When comfort forced her out of herself and she thought of death, she would be like her cats, she would move a little, settle down further, sit in her green armchair and read her newspapers, her books, coming up with ideas for writing, most of which would never take shape.

She was feeling the beginning of discomfort when the phone rang.

"Hi, it's Rose, your neighbour."

A voice behind Rose's, Charles' voice, speaking to someone who wasn't Rose, touched Julie. It added to his smile the last time they saw each other.

"Yes? Everything's all right?"

"I was wondering if you were free to talk. Among neighbours, you know. I've got an idea for a documentary."

Rose's voice was slightly slurred by alcohol, she had that drawl Julie immediately recognized.

"Wait…like now? I'm not sure…"

"It won't take long," Rose cut her off. "I've got a scoop for you."

IV

A FAMILY OUTING

THE TWO WOMEN were facing each other on the roof. They were seated at a wooden picnic table painted bright orange, so orange it reached toward the blue sky with not a cloud in sight. Rose brought a bucket of ice with her, a bottle of white wine, and two large wine glasses. It was the same Chardonnay from Plan B, to Julie's despair who felt the desire to drink come over her. Julie had no defence against alcohol that had once again become—in no time at all, or in the time it took her to pass Charles in the street and talk with him—a force of attraction drawing her in, dark with sudden gaiety, induced relief at a steep price. The bottle brought everything back to her, it was a crystal ball that predicted the steps that led to her fall, the unravelling of this new wound she knew too well, in the heart of a blue afternoon.

Curiously, the railing hadn't been repaired, and disembowelled, it offered a death threat, a promise of destruction to those who stepped too close. Five metres from the table, it opened its maw wide, blackened by lightning. It was almost beautiful in this world obsessed with rules, Julie thought, this northern life mortified by risk, modernity that never missed an opportunity to illustrate potentially dangerous scenarios, always with a certain relish, by the lack of real dangers in its environment. Rose was watching Julie with a sad smile on her face, behind pink sunglasses as garish as the orange of the table and the blue of the sky, where a cloud had appeared, out of nowhere.

Despite the fever beginning to take hold of her, she noticed and studied Rose's lips that had been touched up: slightly swollen, perfectly defined, with expertise, covered with natural beige lipstick, a fleshy mouth, a sweet almond.

"Who did your lips? They're amazing."

Rose put the bottle in the ice bucket and looked up at Julie, involuntarily tightening her lips, suddenly she wanted to hide them.

"I know a lot of surgeons in Montreal," Julie added, looking over the rest of Rose's body, as if to get the latest news.

Rose was shocked. No one had ever called her out on her lips that she got touched up twice a year, no one had ever thrown it into her face, even in the fashion industry where plastic surgery was routine, with the operations that made it what it was. Going to the surgeon was like getting an abortion, the parts put in or taken out were your own and didn't concern anyone else, a personal choice over your own body that you could make completely freely, without justification or negotiation. The results were made to be seen, but that didn't mean they could be discussed, her lips that could be seen by all didn't mean you could talk about them, it didn't mean that her lips—that she hoped would be remarkable—weren't her intimate property, like a toothbrush or a tampon at the bottom of her handbag.

"My lips, yes... I go to Gagnon, Dr. Marc Gagnon."

"I noticed your breasts too, they're really well done too. A bit too high maybe? Though not really, they'll droop with age."

Rose was embarrassed, surprised at what she was hearing and annoyed at losing control of the conversation even before it started. She perceived Julie's head-on impudence dished out as if it were nothing at all as a means of seduction she herself didn't possess, and Julie, who wasn't at all embarrassed by Rose's embarrassment, waited for the rest as she observed her glass held high, at the tip of her fingers, transparency filled with loving liquor against the backdrop of a blue sky, thinking about the cigarette she didn't have, whose taste would have gone so well with the wine.

"There's something people don't see and that I see," Rose began. "It concerns unhappiness in love. It has nothing to do with the so-called incompatible psychologies of men and women."

"It's the foundering of morality, and religion, and authority that transcends the duration of the original infatuation, no? The disappearance of all values that might supplant sexual desire?"

Rose wasn't expecting that sort of reply, and she wasn't sure she understood what it meant. She turned the wine in her glass, describing small staccato circles until a few drops flew out and spattered the table. Despite herself Julie felt the waste, the loss of joy.

"No, no, that's not it... nothing to do with that. Nothing to do with religion or the disappearance of... whatever. Even less with men's feelings that are never as intense. Nor feminism. It's a lot simpler, it's statistical. An aberration, but you can't do anything about it. Not yet. Not today, and not tomorrow."

Julie was in line for a bad time, she understood now. Rose didn't want to talk about subjects for a documentary, but about her and Charles. She wanted to talk about her own situation and their little hobbling triangle through the intermediary of some global vision about the misery of love whose single cause everyone had been searching for since the beginning of time, as if unhappiness wasn't the foundation of love itself.

The sun began to burn the two women like a punishment. In the blue sky a group of white clouds had formed out of nothing, out of itself, begetting made possible by its own potential.

As Rose refilled her glass, Julie inspected her handbag for the cigarette she knew she didn't have. Handbags are often searched by women, she noticed, like a magical and prolific object that produced lost or inexistent objects: money, credit cards, cigarettes, and medication that appeared out of a void that neighboured reality where all the lost things in the world waited, building up in numbers until a few were transmuted into women's handbags, inside their little zippered pockets.

She was searching through her bag when Rose took out an unopened pack of cigarettes, its plastic wrapping untouched, Benson & Hedges Ultra Light King Size, Julie's brand when she was a serious smoker. With that, Rose destabilized Julie, who suddenly understood that Rose had begun to know her in her tastes and habits, she knew how to read her actions, she pre-empted her desires, she saw her when she thought she was alone, when she felt for the edges of her being in her private place. Where had she gotten this information? Probably on the Plan B patio when Rose was listening to her and Charles.

It wasn't Rose spying on her life that troubled Julie the most. The golden pack of cigarettes shining on the orange table brought back the memory of a horrible night at the Assommoir when she offered a flower to a young woman, a blond, whom

Steve was seeing after he'd left her. Having drunk too much, Julie had a revelation. She must immediately execute a symbolic gesture of submission and honour, follow an animal code that all gregarious individuals obey to know their place in the world, she had to act to respect the changing hierarchy of the strong and the weak, the great and the small, to follow the rituals of group survival. It was clear to her that night at the Assommoir that she had to change her impotence into an active role, and find a way to keep her chin up, but she had only humiliated herself further. The bitch of a woman she had secretly nicknamed Girly was embarrassed, Steve even more so; they already felt pity for her because the flower represented even worse initiatives she might undertake, she might fall even lower. A flower or a pack of cigarettes as a way to remain relevant, the proof of her existence in other people's lives, but also a break with common language, the final stage of all communication between victors and vanquished.

After that night at the Assommoir, Steve understood he shouldn't encourage Julie by speaking to her, he even stopped acknowledging her when he saw her out of fear of unleashing a new parade with new antics. His final retreat from mutual recognition, the consensus of a shared past, had been Steve's last demonstration of love for Julie. He didn't want to let her sully herself, Julie decided, didn't want his memory of her dragging through the mud before him, he who had once known her so proud.

As Rose kept her own counsel, Julie told herself that compassion—which only appears when we see ourselves in someone else—was based on egoism; the greater the pain at seeing yourself in another person, the greater the compassion;

the greatest part of compassion was the deep-set horror in your-self that you saw surface in someone else, knowing you could be next. Only in the awareness that you'd stooped as low as the person before you, at least once in your life, could peace be achieved; peace corresponded to the moments of camaraderie in the mutual recognition of humiliation.

Rose remained silent as she watched Julie unwrap the pack of cigarettes with exasperating slowness. Finally, she spoke.

"Love is more difficult for women because they're more nu-merous then men. Leftover women create tension in other women by wanting to carve out a spot with a man. By being too numerous, they jostle for position to be in a relationship. Jostling for position becomes their destiny in love. It's as sim-ple as that."

Julie heard Rose but said nothing, contemplating her own nightmare that evening at the Assommoir through the pack she had finally managed to open, taking out a cigarette and lighting it. As she smoked, she watched bouquets of white clouds forming here and there with worrisome swiftness in the sky over greater Montreal, the North American capital of global warming.

"In Quebec, there are one million women too many, more or less. The population is fluid, it moves from place to place, we shift and it's hard to get a clear view of the crowd. We don't notice it. We don't think about it. We never see it as a problem that affects society as a whole. This million or so extra women create pressure on men, their heads spin with so many women. They don't complain about it, of course. But not knowing where to turn makes them dizzy."

Rose showed no sign of inebriation as Julie slowly felt the

alcohol rise in her. Rose watched the broken guardrail a moment, as if to slough off the weight of all those extra women by pushing them off the roof.

"Men aren't polygamous by nature but they get that way to respond to the pressure women put on them. Contrary to what people think, men are far more in demand than women. There are far more single women than men."

"Impossible," Julie interrupted. "If there were a million more women in Quebec than men, we'd hear about it. Am I right?"

"Why would we hear about it? Neither men nor women see a problem. Men come out on top, they can choose from a wide range of women. Men don't speak out against favourable conditions. That's just instinct."

As she spoke, Rose took the bottle of Chardonnay out of the ice bucket and replaced it, automatically, without even looking at it.

"Women can't draw the link between this reality and the problems in their love life. The fact that they're single more often than not, that they're always being dropped for someone else, women or other men. It's discrimination if you talk about it! It's sexist if you present it as a social problem! Saying it is dangerous in our world. Because of past domination, because of History."

"Okay, okay," Julie said, filling up her glass with what was left of the wine. "Presented like that, it's a big problem. But I can't understand why this disproportion doesn't get more attention. These days everyone's on the lookout for anything out of the ordinary."

"What's strange is that people think the opposite is true, that on Earth there are only men. Just because it's the case on television, in the news, in politics, everywhere. All your history books, war in the Middle East, in the Arab countries, in Africa, everyone we hear and see, they're all men. Global history is saturated with men. Women are invisible except in ads and videos. Or on the Internet, where they're overflowing."

"Okay, I follow you, but what you're saying is outrageous. In China and India, there are mass killings of girls by way of abortion and murder. You do know that, right?"

"Yes. In countries like China and India there are millions of women missing. One hundred million in all. Because of large-scale foeticides and infanticides. But the massacre of girls makes people think that there are not enough women elsewhere in the world. It's the opposite."

Rose was beginning to grab Julie's attention; she was beautiful in her enthusiasm, not a rigid, frozen beauty but something alive, she was turning into a real person, glowing and baroque, the kind Julie liked. And there was some truth in what she was saying, Julie thought, a truth announced with pompousness, a way of revealing the underlying drama by dishonestly exaggerating the distribution of gender, which Julie liked, it reminded her of Charles' father's Amazons with their pussy-eyes.

"Okay, let's say you're right, but what are you referring to? A study? Something on TV?"

"In Quebec and everywhere else in the West, the population is 52% women. Anyone can verify that. Those are UN official statistics. Of seven million people in Quebec, that adds up to 280,000 women too many. It doesn't seem like much but there's something else that makes all the difference. Fifteen percent of men are gay, at least. I say at least because I'm an optimist. So maybe more. Some studies show that up to 20% are gay. But let's be optimistic: 15% of men are gay, meaning

504,000 gays in Quebec. If you subtract those men who aren't interested in women from the total, there are only 2,856,000 men who love women and want to form relationships with them. So 784,000 men are missing. Which makes 784,000 women too many. Almost a million."

For Rose to know those statistics by heart impressed Julie, who understood nothing about numbers because they didn't follow any aesthetic logic and did nothing more than force the mind to consider a specific catastrophic reality. The outrageous numbers and statistics and percentages made her head spin when she tried to face the reality Rose was trying to describe, though she succeeded only in making it threatening and vague. Julie was lost. The only thing she understood was that Rose was preparing some possibility that would probably become real.

She knew that there were more women than men in the West, and in Africa it was truer, since they represented 60% of the population according to what she'd heard on the television. She also had the impression that homosexuality was growing among men, and had noticed that the more women in any given society walked around in states of undress, the more they flaunted their bodies, the more men turned from them to desire each other. The more women offered themselves, the more men refused what was being offered—freely and easily, what's more. But to that extent? Could the epidemic of short relationships, breakups, and divorces be linked to a numerical disadvantage between men and women, made more extreme by male homosexuality?

"What about lesbians?"

"There aren't enough. Less than 1% of women are gay."

"Lesbians are as numerous as gays. We think there are less

of them because they're not as visible. They don't display themselves as much, or go out as much, or talk as much. That's what they say. That's what I've heard. It's what everyone says."

Suddenly offended, Rose jumped to her feet, onto her high heels, jostling the table and her wine glass that tipped over in a small puddle and a tinkling of glass. She stood out against the changing sky that reminded Julie of the one that had spat down lightning that struck the guardrail.

"There aren't as many because there aren't as many! I don't care what everyone says!"

Rose's entire face and body were caught up in torment. It turned her words into a staccato stutter. Everything about her required attention and submission, listening to her wasn't a choice but the price to pay to be in her presence.

"There are way, way less," she continued, sitting down without righting her glass that Julie kept staring at.

"That's just the way it is. You can't compare male and female homosexuality. Think about it. You meet gays every day in the street, in the shops, at the hairdresser's, on television, every day, every day! I'm sure you know some, you've known plenty in your life, dozens and dozens, maybe hundreds. At the gay pride parades, only gay men! In the gay neighbourhoods, only gay men! Just look! Look and see for yourself!"

Rose pointed her index finger at the sky as if the parades and gay neighbourhoods she was talking about were to be found there, with their excesses of flesh and colour, their sequined, sparkled wriggling, their floats covered with cocks and muscles. But there were only cottony white and grey clouds that seemed to rush down toward the roof, filling the air with humidity that stuck to the flesh like leprosy.

"Okay, Rose, I admit it, it's obvious, irrefutable. These days we're so obsessed with gender equality that we stick it where it doesn't belong. We think of equality as symmetry, which is foolish."

Rose wasn't listening to Julie, Rose wasn't even speaking to her, Rose was trying to settle the score far beyond Julie. She was declaring her opposition to the world at large, her refusal of the established order of things.

"Do you know a lot of lesbians? Do you have any among your friends? Have you ever had one in your life? Real lesbians, not the ones that make out with their drunk friends in bars to show off and be sexy. Not the ones that think they're bisexual because they messed around, or wanted to mess around with another woman. Or the ones that are bored enough to sleep with other women without coming or getting wet just so they can talk about it afterwards. To impress their friends. For the pleasure of saying it, you understand?"

In the distance, a rumbling of thunder was heard, a single growl, confusion in the sky that didn't know which leg to stand on, it was dropping into its lower keys like a piano. No one could tell which direction the sky would take.

"Since when do women show off less than men? Or talk less than them? That's all women do! Talk about themselves and reveal themselves, their interior, their emotions. Women and their sentimental truths! Women and their need to say everything! Bitches! Whores!"

With these words Julie woke up for real, this was getting serious. Rose had stopped beating around the bush, she'd touched the heart of the subject: scheming. Rose had rarely talked so much in her life, and all of sudden she realized she should stop there. She confessed more than she should have, just as Charles had done a few days earlier. She gushed on the roof in front of Julie—whom Charles liked so much, she could no longer ignore it—the deepest, most painful part of herself, she showed the irregular cloth from which her life was cut. But at least she'd done it, she consoled herself, without speaking of her father to Julie, that man she had loved with such passion, the likes of which only children are capable of. That father had disappointed her, and she had him in the back of her mind as she was speaking.

Julie said nothing for fear of arousing Rose further, for her anger seemed to be diminishing. Then Rose sat back at the table, crossed her legs, and placed a hand on her hip. She pulled the bottle of wine out of the bucket for the second time, and seeing it was empty, violently dropped it back in. Julie, Rose's audience, drew a line between the threatening sky and her ferocity, and she hoped only for a return to a calmer climate. She lit another cigarette.

"There isn't a single reason why women would be bashful about coming out of the closet," Rose continued. "There's no reason, at least today, in our society, to hide it if they were. They don't hide because the truth is that they aren't!"

"No, Rose, no reason at all."

Rose stood up again. Getting her second wind, she began pacing around the table.

"There are so few of them that it's an injustice to all women! If only they had an alternative to being lesbian! But no, they belong only to men and to men only!"

Rose went on punishing the roof with her heels, a prisoner of her speech, unable to find the exit. She couldn't stop and she couldn't continue. She served up her pain at being in the world without relief, in its reality forged of flaws, of existences unbidden in the same sandbox, on the same territory, condemned to remove themselves from life or, worse, share it. That pain had been contained in darkness for the longest time, years of fermenting in explanations of misery, years of resistance, of stubborn acceptance of gangrened excuses that now burst in the light of day.

"It's the tension between women! That's the problem! The tension of having to fight like a bitch to keep a man!"

Rose sat back down and looked Julie in the eye to make her presence felt, there, before her. Tension was a problem, Julie thought, Rose was right. Tension like a dynamic of pain and the movement toward succour, tension that she had tried to reduce, prevent it from re-entering her sleepy life in any way possible, tension like a starter's pistol for pain, a signal to move and raise your fists and fight, give into panic that tried only to reduce its source, and get back to the level, slow plane of quietude, Nirvana where life was unmoving, flattened out, like death. Tension at the origin of life was also life that had to be tamed.

Rose looked into Julie's eyes and said, "Charles is mine."

Charles...let her keep Charles, Julie thought, happy to feel that Rose, by finally naming him, had reached the end of herself. Julie took a violet felt-tip pen and a piece of paper out of her handbag, and wrote something. She handed the paper to Rose.

"Send me the data, numbers, and statistics comparing the birth of boys and girls. Births according to gender, as well as homosexuality. To this email. I want to study them. What you're telling me seems incredible. But for now we're out of wine."

The sky was covered with drifting clouds. An ambulance

wailed down Saint Joseph Boulevard, going west. Rose smiled, appeased, her mouth like a sweet balm that shone.

"Want to go to Plan B?"

TAWNY FUR, INTERMIXED with beige and brown, Chafouin, Julie's largest and laziest cat, was the first thing she saw when she opened her eyes burnt by excess, the next day around noon. He was sleeping next to her in a ball, entombed in his six kilos, his nose on his back legs bent back toward him in that classic pose of every cat in the world, bastard or not. Feeling Julie move, he opened his eyes, then closed them with a sigh. For him, nothing out of the ordinary had occurred, his world had stayed the same, life continued its course, without past or future, a dog's life, without the beatings.

For a few seconds after she woke, Julie remembered nothing of the previous night and it was far better that way. Memory had its reasons for forgetting things that concerned well-being and self-esteem, forgetting was a gift from heaven that locked up the filth and threw away the key.

There was no clarity in her mind, only pain and dryness that obscured her vision. Knowing she was in her own house was the only thing that counted, being at home and not naked, at least not entirely. She was lying on her stomach on top of her undisturbed bed, her feet on the pillow. Her jeans were where they should be, attached at her waist by a large black leather belt, but her T-shirt was pushed over her breasts. Then as sure as the sun rises in the morning to throw its light over all Creation, the night's memories began to return.

"Oh, no! Shit! Shit shit shit!"

The events, convivial at first, had gone too far. As usual, as usual, she repeated, raising herself on her elbows and scanning her loft to make sure everything was still in place, that the material stability of her life in its incarnations of furniture and electronics, its proliferation of green plants and walls covered in pictures and paintings, hadn't gone anywhere, hadn't—as she had—forgotten themselves by letting loose in every direction at once. Julie didn't worry too much about herself, protected by so many nights far worse, passed out in the arms of strangers, or waking up outside the city in a puddle of urine.

She had to get up. Lifting herself on her elbows, she immediately located her white satin bra on the wooden floor, the one she'd been wearing last night, except that the straps had been undone. A bit farther off, her gold leather handbag was on its side, spitting out makeup, coins, balled up Kleenex, and business cards she'd picked up in the course of the evening. Then, near the mess of her handbag, she recognized a belt, it too made of black leather: Charles' belt.

"Goddamn shit. He forgot it."

Other memories returned, linked to the belt left on the floor and her t-shirt raised over her breasts which she pulled back down, muttering, the action was immediately followed by a searing pain in her head where static crackled, probably the noise of the circuits in her brain trying to rediscover lost pathways. Julie got out of the bed and stumbled toward the shower, to avoid letting images parade by that might have been exciting if her mind hadn't been clouded by a headache, if she hadn't been so hungover, if the images hadn't included Rose as a witness. She shrieked in rage as she accidentally turned on the cold water. Her three cats leaped to their feet in unison, their ears turning in her direction, eager not to miss anything of the fury that reached them from the shower.

At Plan B, Rose and Julie had continued drinking white wine, the same Chardonnay neither of them would drink after Charles' death, neither would be able to see a bottle of it on the liquor store shelf without recoiling.

Seated on the always jam-packed patio, Julie was amazed to gaze upon—for the first time—the world described by Rose twenty minutes earlier on the roof of the building: of the thirty-nine customers seated outside, twenty-eight were women, and of the sixty or so inside the bar, according to Rose's and Julie's approximate count that kept getting disrupted by the comings and goings of customers who gawked at them, forty were women. Julie had always thought of masculine presence as domination through physical force and numbers, domination through the colossal buildup which men were capable of in time of war and popular uprisings, for Julie who never lacked men to hold her in their arms, it was hard to believe. Julie was seeing for the first time what had been there all along, she'd been troubled enough to approach groups of women over the evening and ask them whether they had noticed this reality, whether they were bothered by it, worried or revolted. Most of them, like Julie, were looking and seeing for the first time. Most didn't know what to think, they believed it was just coincidence, a random occurrence that had brought more women than usual together, at the same time they recognized having sensed this reality in some dim fashion without wanting to notice or reflect on it. Julie was amazed to realize, in her thirty-third year, that she'd never noticed the distribution of the sexes in the places she patronized and that she'd never, ever considered the repercussions of this mathematical distribution on the hardships of love, and the cliché of women waiting for men gone off hunting, outside, elsewhere.

"It's always like that," Rose told her, gloating at how the fact rattled her. "I've been noticing it for so many years that I can't unsee it. In all Montreal, the Plateau is the neighbourhood where the concentration of women is the highest. But you should see what it's like in Saguenay Lac-Saint-Jean. The statistics aren't entirely clear, but according to the darkest predictions, there are seven women for every man."

"Really? I thought that was a myth."

"It's true. Completely true. I don't know why or how. In any case, the worst places are restaurants, in Montreal and elsewhere. Women go out in packs in restaurants, it's striking. The worst was at Bu, a tapas place. I checked the place a couple of times. Only women, forty-three of them. And one man. Only one!"

And since they mentioned the tapas at Bu, the two women agreed they should eat something if they wanted to continue drinking. They swallowed down all sorts of pâtés on toast, black olives and shrimp mousse, nuts and goat cheese and more bread, leaving out the wine just long enough to get their strength back. They spoke of other things, the sweltering summer in their country of snow, the World Cup that they both couldn't be bothered with except that it assembled men in great packs, their common experience of aesthetic obsession that Julie had long considered a sort of Western burqa. The aesthetic fixation, Julie submitted, covered the body with a veil of constraints spun with extraordinary expenditures of time and money, hopes and disillusions vanquished by new products and techniques, operations and touch-ups that cloaked the body in superimposed layers, until the body was eclipsed. It was a veil both transparent and dishonest that denied the physical truth it claimed it was revealing, in the place of real skin it inserted skin without faults, hermetic, inalterable, a cage.

"They're Vulva-Women," she repeated, an expression of the moment that made them laugh. "Vulva-Women are entirely covered with their own pussies, they disappear behind them."

Rose didn't always understand Julie, and Julie, who kept complimenting Rose for everything and nothing and even her silence, who took her hands in hers and sung her praises thick with inebriation, revealed her recent past by telling the story of her disappointments in love, her collapse that, she had to admit, wasn't entirely over since she was still drinking, because she'd never be the same with alcohol or men, because she rediscovered the desire to live without really finding life. Then Bertrand appeared on the patio, he sat down and began drinking with them, he tried his luck with Julie and then with Rose, his manoeuvres were rejected by both women, teasing accomplices.

The rest of the evening was lost in a haze dominated by a few images separated from the pack, but that were themselves ambiguous. Julie saw herself simultaneously in two different bars, the Assommoir and the Tap Room, without knowing which came first. She saw herself in a disorder of time and space, a collision of images, taking Rose by the hand and walking with her, kissing Rose on the mouth in front of a dumbstruck Bertrand. Then she saw Charles arriving and Rose moving away from her, she saw herself looking for cocaine, finding some, not having enough money to pay for it, then finding some way anyway, moving toward the washroom with first Rose then Charles, but much later, kissing Charles on the mouth, in the toilet, lifting her T-shirt at her house, feeling Charles' hands on her breasts, without knowing if it was at the bar or at home, feeling his mouth, trying to touch his cock in his jeans, his belt undone. She saw her cats on the bed disturbed by the mechanical animation of pleasure, the mess of caresses indistinguishable from previous nights with other men. She recalled Rose appearing next to the bed, mirror image of her safari-dress appearance in front of Plan B's cedar hedge, a terrible apparition that slowly came into view, where they had been seen far more than they saw.

Julie pictured herself walking through the streets with the troupe though realizing Rose was standing alone, not looking at anyone, because of Charles being all over her, Julie, who couldn't stop talking. She remembered Rose disappearing with Bertrand once they had gotten back to the building on Colonial Avenue, and Charles staying with her to talk and talk, drink more and snort a little, for an uncertain length of time that seemed both very long and very short.

There were all sorts of things she couldn't remember and that worried her, like the sexual contact that left her with a feeling of coldness and strangeness, bodies thrashing against each other short-circuited by everything that was poisoning her blood. Curiously, Charles' cock didn't make an appearance, maybe because Charles hadn't let Julie touch it, or because he couldn't get hard. She had no memory of when Charles and Rose left her loft, or his reaction when they'd been caught by Rose, nor could she remember how Rose reacted.

She forgot how she'd managed to pay for the cocaine and in what quantity, but she retained an image in which she was licking the bottom of a plastic baggie. She saw Rose and recalled the two of them dragging each other through the Tap Room, hand in hand, to contemplate the miracle of a majority of men in the crowd, a late night influx that had thrilled them and led them to produce a lesbian comedy of deep kisses on the mouth, but she couldn't remember the path they'd taken to the bar. She remembered the late-night appearance of a producer she had worked with in the past and had forgotten why he told her he never wanted to work with her again, or why she'd kept a bunch of his business cards.

Julie got out of the shower, covered herself with a clean towel, pulled the drapes, and settled back into bed, under the covers. Her body was filled with a deep shame, shame at her actions but also at everyone else in the world who acted the way she had. She was ashamed of herself, and of this world where everything was allowed, where permissiveness turned life into infection, and clouded it with stink. Shame of her adolescence that continued into adulthood, the prime of her life where she should have been somewhere else entirely, in discipline and work, the will to choose a path and direction, accomplishment and a quest for recognition, progress with a mind turned toward marking History, the need to leave a mark on the world. She of this self-indulgence that was growing in her, senescence like an insouciant giant, an ungainly beast unaware of the damage left by its passing. Ashamed too was she of her generation's veneration of pleasure that made everything possible and acceptable as long as it was light and frivolous, as long as it was birthed in the heart and came from the gut, as long as it could be turned into a joke around the table during a dinner party with friends. Ashamed of the alcohol that rotted her, that transformed her into something else, a cow, a sow, a savage state where she snorted and displayed herself like a bitch in heat. She was ashamed of her vulgarity in which the vulgarity of the times was reflected, she was ashamed of all the moments when she simply felt no shame. Prone in her bed, she concluded that shame always came too late, always the next day, and never came when it should have, when it was needed, when it should hurry to be felt to prevent the worst, but it didn't intervene, at least not in time. Then she figured that the times she acted like a sow were the only ones when she was part of the world. Shame was separation, and acting like a sow was union, public defecation.

Under the covers, as always Julie contemplated the ceiling, and felt her desire for Charles intact. She felt it in her fear of having disappointed him, or driven him away with her prattling, her cocaine-induced enthusiasm, synaptic joy, her extravagant mannerisms and declarations about the world, her shamelessness that opened her up like a door. Her desire was intact because she wanted to see Charles and make sure, despite everything, that he still found her beautiful.

Men, she had come to see, remain brothers before the vulgarity of men, but are nauseated when women act the same way, women shouldn't drink beer straight from the bottle according to her father, shouldn't curse, women had to be discreet to a fault, especially when it came to their mouths. It was a matter of habit and time, Julie thought, you had to give the world time to adapt so that the equality of men and women in filth came naturally to everyone's senses like a state of nature.

Julie knew her mind wouldn't stop, it was a stranger to both exhaustion and pity, but she fell back to sleep anyway, with images of Charles.

She woke up eight hours later, Chafouin's nose tickling her neck.

V

THE WAR EFFORT

ROSE DUBOIS WAS sitting in a waiting room on Beaubien Street, with ads running on a television set high in the top corner of the room, like a professor at a lectern. Bitchiness had been part of her life for several days now, since she caught Charles and Julie together on Plan B's patio, and it seemed to want to make a definite place for itself in her life. The feeling said it all, it was an established state of being. Her universe was caught up in bitchiness, all Plateau Mont-Royal and her work even more so, including this waiting roomed filled with female customers flipping through fashion magazines waiting for their wrinkles to be needled away, consulting promotional leaflets for Botox, Restylane, Dermadeep, Artecoll, and other new products whose many advantages Rose hadn't discovered yet.

Like the other women, she was waiting in this room decorated in lush complementary tones of green and yellow, filled with everything that existed in the name of well-being, value added, extra self-confidence provided by injection, the gifts you gave yourself, for yourself and no one else, you could read that in the ads, one of which trumpeted the slogan *For me, me, me*. Plastic surgery is somehow centripetal, autarkic, Rose told herself, as she waited like the other women for the same thing they were waiting for, sitting in the antechamber of every wound required in the name of beauty, pain migrating toward the marvellous like so many caterpillars, after gestation, guaranteed to turn into colourful butterflies, yet that still needed a new boost every six months to keep their colour and stay aflutter.

Rose managed to find a replacement at work and Charles understood why, he respected her reasons, and even offered to give her a week off work—a first in their work relationship. He was kind to her because he loved the swelling that hardened her lips when she emerged from the surgeon's clinic, kind with her lips that he nibbled on carefully in the days following her operation, his hand running back and forth over his cock until he came on her lips, then spread his sperm over them with the tip of his cock like in a porn movie. Kind in his uncontrollable excitement and stubborn erection, or so thought Rose who considered his offer of a week off as a way of pushing her aside, of laying her off, of wanting her to get used to being independent and saving her from sensing him drawing away from her. That he cared for her as he put distance between them made her suffer that much more and she couldn't comprehend why, maybe because his niceties only dragged out her pain, prolonged the torture, washed the guilty party of his sins. She had contradictory thoughts: nothing had happened yet between Charles and Julie because everything was still ambiguous, but everything would happen because of that ambiguity, that much more powerful because it floated above them instead of consuming itself and breaking apart, that hesitation was enough for her to establish the truth, a truth of the heart. Rose felt she should leave to avoid humiliation, at the same time she needed to stay and resist, and experience humiliation to the end, turn it back on them, humiliate herself to piss them off, make a splash, keep the malaise alive, stick around like a bad apple in their projects and maybe just destroy them. Stay in the picture not to see, but to make them see her.

Rose looked at the women who were waiting along with her, women of all ages with their eyes on the pages of magazines made for them, bursting with products designed for their needs. Only women, once again. Then a man on the road to becoming something other than a man, the by-product of a man mutating into a woman, walked into the waiting room, eyes slightly closed by the swelling that was healing, with fading bruises, yellow and violet, on his cheeks. He was wearing a medical mask over his mouth indicating that something had happened at that level that shouldn't be seen. The man, who wore prosthetic breasts, had square shoulders that didn't fit in with what he wanted to be, poor guy, not to mention that he was too tall, with strong features impossible to erase, his hips too narrow under the skirt that ended above his knees, that revealed his legs that were too muscled, and his calves that were too big, those two parts could not—at least not yet—be reduced to something more refined and slender.

Rose wondered whether he still had a cock and couldn't help but think, *one more too many*. Then she corrected herself and thought again: too bad for this middle-of-the-fencer, I feel sorry for him for wanting to be a woman, knowing that's impossible, neither men nor women, and homosexuals even less, no matter their gender, will want this synthetic creature that has lost or soon will lose its gender, but that will retain the indicators of it for the rest of his life on the remains of his body, despite all his life's work.

Then she thought of Isabelle, a svelte model of Italian origin, a woman who'd become her good friend for a while, a few years back. The image of Isabelle arose to refute her thoughts, without dissuading her from her beliefs. When it came to her theories, Rose had an obstinate streak, what couldn't be hammered out grossly and before the eyes of all didn't count, for her truth had no nuances and was always ironclad, it didn't float into the people's minds, it didn't illuminate but was a blow to the head, the nature of truth was crushing.

Isabelle had told her the details of her life in Madrid where she went from time to time to model, but mostly to whore, as she had done in Montreal, London, and Paris. Her stories were always worth your while. In the flesh market, she had rubbed shoulders with transsexuals who—to Rose's real surprise for she didn't want to believe it—got paid more than real women, even the youngest who were most in demand all over the globe. Transsexuals whose transformation had been a success, and who all looked like one another because they'd been recast by the same Madrid surgeons, all of them with the same eyebrows, high and oblique, that made them look as though they were forever casting a downward glance on you, their mouths like an ampulla, a pussy right in their faces, enormous breasts, double D, E, F. Well, Isabelle maintained, they made a fortune with clients who weren't homosexuals, men who were able to get it up not only for their joke toward which their cocks had turned, but who preferred the hybrid gender to the real one. Isabelle described the ambiguous results of some of the transformations she'd seen: folds of flesh made from the testicles themselves, folds that looked like a dick, and balls, she said, describing the results with the rounded palm of her hand, results that looked like attempts at pussies that had neither the proportion, colour, and even less the texture of the real thing. Transsexuals had mitigated genitals, Isabelle would say ironically, when she was in a good mood. Of the infinite varieties of pussy in the world and their idiosyncrasies, a transsexual's cock folded back into itself shouldn't even be mentioned in the same category. The dry, arid hole that often wasn't more than fifteen centimetres couldn't come close to a real hole, yet men would get hard and pay top dollar to fuck it.

That just goes to show how nature is unnecessary when it comes to erections, Rose thought as she listened to Isabelle, who'd gotten hitched to some British photographer, or so she'd heard not long ago. Every year Isabelle would send her an electronic birthday card that danced and played dreary music over and over again, on a loop.

Rose couldn't stop looking at the transsexual, she stared at him with merciless curiosity, so intense it was odious. She was still looking at him when Dr. Gagnon appeared in the waiting room, the only man in the troop of appellants, to motion Rose to follow him into his office. He was used to seeing Rose on a regular basis and was starting to feel a certain warmth toward her. He had noticed that the younger his patients were, the more often they came to visit him, maybe because they'd heard their mothers endlessly repeat that it was better to be safe than sorry. Getting a leg up on old age, he understood, yielded more than the bandages that sought to hide it.

Dr. Gagnon was a handsome forty-five-year-old with a big smile who preferred Rose over his other patients for reasons he couldn't quite explain. He was touched by her fragile nature, she was so small you could do what you wanted to her. That thought was a source of pleasure for him, he imagined grabbing her and pulling her to his side with violent kisses, or throwing her out the window, against the wall, until she begged and pleaded. Dr. Gagnon couldn't decide which of these brutal scenarios he preferred.

Rose sat across from him, in his position behind the solid, serious doctor's desk.

"Haven't seen you in a while, Rose. All's well with you?"

Dr. Gagnon knew she could read his thoughts on his face, so he turned to the reports of her recent visits, remembering with some embarrassment that in the past few months, she'd been coming much too often, he had seen her only three weeks ago to freeze the muscles of her forehead and the skin around her eyes with Botox.

"Things are okay here," she answered, pointing at her forehead with her index finger. "I showed up out of the blue because I wanted a little more... for my mouth... to highlight it, to showcase it, you know?"

"Of course, yes, of course... come a little closer," he asked, opening his hands and making Rose get up and bend over his desk.

Dr. Gagnon examined her lips with his both thumbs. They were to his liking on every level, and they made him want to fill them with himself. But the perfect lips she showed him were perceived, by the typical woman she was, not as a feature she should derive pleasure from, but as material that could be moulded indefinitely and pushed endlessly toward improvement.

"I guess we could aim for a bit more volume on the upper and lower, by injecting in the middle, in small doses, to thicken them. A single syringe, I wouldn't recommend more than that."

"I want my lips to pop," she insisted, sitting back down and lifting one hand in front of her mouth, as if to shield them from him.

"They'll pop, they'll pop. But always harmoniously."

"I trust you to use gentle aggression, Doctor."

Her reply had Dr. Gagnon laughing, but his laughter was much too high-pitched and enthusiastic, it was heard throughout the clinic, and his bored assistants rolled their eyes toward the ceiling. Then his laughter dropped off suddenly, leaving them both embarrassed and facing each other. Rose knew that her surgeon had a weakness for her, she used that to her advantage, but this was the first time she felt like letting him near her, to bring him closer to what was happening to her, the emptiness she saw opening before her.

"I think my boyfriend is going to leave me. For a woman in our building," she burst out, mortified by the tears welling up in her eyes.

Usually, and with someone else, Dr. Gagnon would have side-stepped the confession with a polite smile and a courteous attitude that left no doubt he wasn't there to discuss his patients' private lives. Too many women confessed far too easily in his office, believing there was necessarily an intimate relationship between doctor and patient because he would open them up, turn them inside out and restyle them. But this was Rose, and what he heard were dulcet tones indeed: this was the first time she shared something intimate with him.

"He's crazy to even think about it," the doctor declared.

"We just moved in together. And we work together. It's the other woman…"

Rose was about to burst into tears and fall apart in her surgeon's office, she tried to stave off her broken-hearted bitch howl by turning and staring at the wall full of diplomas that she couldn't read, then moving onto black and white portraits of women from the Roaring Twenties, pictures she noticed for the first time. Portraits of glowing ivory faces with liquid eyes, undulating, wavy hair that broke the light like a prism, beautiful silent children whose entire vocabulary was contained in the batting of eyelashes.

"You know that cosmetic surgery can't be used to keep a man. Even if people are led to believe otherwise, it has no effect on lost love. Many women have tried and failed."

"On my man it'll work," Rose replied immediately, in a tone of complete self-assurance. "But I understand what you mean. The other woman, the neighbour, she's my type that way. I wouldn't be surprised if she was your patient too."

Rose didn't know where she was going with Julie, but she couldn't help talking about her, or thinking about her. Having come into her life through Charles, Julie had become unavoidable, inseparable from her own destiny. But did she have to carry her everywhere, even to the surgeon's office, where the shape of her body would be decided?

Dr. Gagnon wanted to continue the conversation, but time was flying, he had to move. He asked Rose to lie down on the operating table as usual, and injected a dose of morphine in her arm as usual, bringing her to the edge of sleep, where in general, life is good, even for the miserable and the diseased. Silence fell throughout the clinic, Rose lay almost asleep before him, he could take the time to examine every inch of her without embarrassment, she was more desirable than ever, Rose the sleeping beauty who needed a mouth to kiss. He took out a syringe, but before he injected her, he took her hand and bent over her, brushing her ear with his lips.

"You'll always be welcome here if you need consolation. Even from the pain given to you by the man you love."

From deep within the peace that ran through her veins, Rose smiled, not knowing whether her smiled really existed or if it was only an intention, the thought of a smile. With the touching ungainliness of very shy people, Dr. Gagnon bent over further and kissed her on the lips before operating on them. He was extremely careful with the procedure, not injecting the whole syringe, to give her what she wanted without destroying what she had.

When Rose felt strong enough to get to her feet and walk out of the clinic without needing to lean on the walls, she emerged from the small recovery room reserved for minor procedures, her mouth covered with a mask, and made her way to reception. Behind her counter a secretary had told her, with a voice better suited for a morgue, her mouth upturned in a haughty sneer, that this time she didn't have to pay.

IN THE TAXi she couldn't stop herself from touching her lips with the tip of her fingers, the swelling of her lips continued, she thought of Charles and his strange desire for this swelling wound. Her surgeon had kissed her on the operating table. He broke the barrier between them in her moment of voluntary submission, as she waited for him to produce what would get Charles excited, as she was trapped, open to his touch. She was aware of it and didn't know what to think. In any case, it was the least of her worries.

An idea was slowly dawning on her, her surgeon was a doctor who might, if she worked on him well enough, operate on her for free the way he had done in the past a few times, and give her, who knows, some money since he had piles of it, not to mention that he might be able to prescribe her all sorts of things difficult to get your hands on, like pain medication and anxiolytics that propel you into deep sleep with no questions asked, pills that heal people whose souls are sick, where putrefaction grows.

Between her and Charles there had never been any great discussions about life. They were both secretive and not very curious about other people, their curiosity wasn't expressed through words but in their sight, well developed by their profession. She sensed Charles more than she understood him, through intuitions she couldn't express in words, she sniffed him out, reacting to his changing moods like a domestic animal, dogs and cats that panic and hide under furniture, whining when they feel a storm coming, or purr and wag their tails. She'd known certain things her whole life, but was only gaining awareness of them now, just as they were about to slip from her grasp.

Rose knew Charles had loved the women in his life serenely, including her, he'd always taken his time, approaching them indirectly or letting them come to him, attentive and patient. She also knew that Charles had never known the all-consuming power of passion, he had always declined the animal aspect of love where you lose yourself like a beast, releasing your instincts on the other person, giving yourself wholly to the chosen one who devours you.

No man in the world loved women more than Charles, she knew this from having lived and worked with him for years, but there were barriers in his love he couldn't overcome, emotions that remained inaccessible, like the torment and pain of jealousy and the violence of possession. He had never seen his world fade into nothing from the physical absence of someone he loved, nor had he lost all interest in anything his lover didn't care for. Rose knew he loved her with that trusting, solid, patient love old couples have.

But beyond what she knew of Charles, Rose believed that Julie O'Brien would be an exception, Rose was beginning to feel the spark of passion in him, something he'd never known. Recently he'd been distracted, clumsy, confused. For the past few weeks she'd felt him ready to follow Julie anywhere at the slightest sign, ready to commit any folly. She saw in Julie the ideal being that she wasn't and that she should have been, with Charles, of course, but also with other men who all sought the Ideal Female, a model etched into their gender since the beginning of time and which they grasped after, a template in their DNA that they followed with their erections, in unison.

But when it came to Charles, Rose still had an advantage that Julie didn't, and it had to do with his cock. He had tastes and preferences that horrified him and that he never spoke off, especially not to Rose who consented in silence. He never spoke of his desires like the good, considerate boy he was. His preferences were the opposite of consideration and sensitivity, they were the very opposite of nature itself, if nature could even be mentioned in that area. His appetite was contrary to all reproductive logic, he believed, and to everything that made him a human being, everything he wanted and wished for himself and others. But don't all appetites lead to the destruction of everything that gets you to open your mouth? Wasn't hunger the negation of food? Isn't nature in large part directed against itself to control its terrible expansion through mechanisms of reabsorption? Sometimes Charles figured that perversion saved men by preventing reproduction through diverting their sperm onto sterile objects that didn't produce ovum, like cadavers, shit, and feet.

But Charles still suffered from a burning desire and a swollen cock for women with breast implants and for bodies that had other bodies in them that didn't belong to them, for swelling lips inflated with fill, lips you could feel with your fingers, your lips, your cock. He felt the same for the scars left like signs of entering, a call to fever, for implants, injected substances, hardening, wounds, injuries of beauty beaten into the body that generated in him such excitement that it had taken him time—weeks—to hold back and keep from shooting his wad as soon as he touched her naked body, he preferred her breasts to her pussy, her lips to her ass. He penetrated her here and there just to please her, and only for the first year of their relationship. Then he'd stopped entirely, understanding that Rose herself had decided to take on the role of pure fetish: made for sex without sex, Charles taking her silence as the confirmation that she really didn't need the kind of penetration that has been universally practiced since the dawn of man.

But that passion, because that's what it was, was the only one he had ever experienced, and it had nothing to do with love, Rose knew. The moment when he was lost to pleasure was short and had a predetermined and abrupt end that left him disconcerted and nauseous, and Rose felt the same, she would look at Charles when fever took him, when he switched without warning from being gentle and caring to abandoning his whole self to a part of her body that couldn't make her come unless she touched herself.

His was a precise performance that almost never varied, he imposed it on her to control and handle her, wanting the rest of her to disappear or at least keep quiet. During his fever, Charles would ignore Rose and manipulate only one part of her, a nipple, for example, the very summit of a certain suspect hardness created by implants, the proof of human intervention, dictated by human desire, a refusal to be only this much, only an "A" on a scale that went much higher, firmness the result of an effort toward something better, a higher state, according to the point of view.

Rose saw Charles for the first time at a photo shoot. Three famous models were there to advertise some new techno club. They had to pose like pussy gone mad for lesbian desire, two of them kissing while the third put her hand in the hollow between her thighs, and her mouth on the second one's breasts.

At the time Rose was a stylist's assistant and Charles an assistant photographer. She was small compared to everyone, and she had a talent for getting out of people's way, moving aside when they had agency, a hidden presence that knows its position in the scale of things: in the periphery. But in her debasement that day, she demonstrated some solidity, pride even, a sort of robustness made possible because she wasn't suffering, she was refusing the humiliation of the three models and their tantrums and whims, who were taking advantage of the group effect there in the studio to complain about their hair, makeup, and clothes.

Rose caught Charles watching her several times. Each time he reacted with a smile in lieu of an excuse, a timid mouth that seemed to say *I can't do anything about it*. Charles absent-mindedly followed the proceedings, moving between the makeup station and the set where the models were waiting, inspecting the photo equipment, the lights, flashes, spots, and silks, the XXX grills, giraffes, and umbrellas, the two assistants quiet as they watched the three women who looked like a litter of kittens covered in pink fabric that Rose and the official stylist had to set up, fold by fold—to make it seem as though it had been tossed there in the heat of passion, in organized negligence.

Once the shoot was over, they found themselves walking side by side in the street. Rose, who was always ready to serve, offered to drive Charles home. As they drove, they spoke very little but Rose felt, with her two small hands gripping the wheel, Charles looking her over from head to toe. Despite his effort to see her body as a whole, he couldn't take his eyes off of the swelling of her lips like a small internal haemorrhage, an obstinate, stubborn mouth, the flesh turned up prettily that made him want to pinch her and arouse pain. He was searching for words to invite her up to his place for a drink, but the closer they came to his house the more the idea began to lose its meaning. Anyway, getting women to fuck him wasn't his thing. Once they were in front of his house, he'd already forgotten her name. He got out of the car and said goodbye, taking with him the picture of her mouth that called out for offence, violation.

Two years went by before they saw each other again, two years during which Charles had become an efficient and well-liked photographer, and she a stylist, sometimes helped by assistants, but mostly working by herself with Laurent, her favourite hairdresser and makeup artist. She liked him a lot because working with him was, as she said, like working with silk.

One day Charles hired Rose without giving it much thought, without knowing who she was, following the recommendation of a colleague who'd left to pursue a career overseas. He had completely forgotten her. But when she showed up in the studio with a man he thought was her boyfriend, he recognized her immediately. She hadn't changed a bit, she was small and delectable, with new curves under her t-shirt, sculpted without exaggeration, just enough to be desired. He'd made the right decision, he figured, and he felt a warm feeling for his photographer friend, and Bertrand, the boyfriend, only made her more desirable. There was no need to hurry, he told himself. He had to remain cautious and bide his time, let their interaction find its hierarchy, and the dynamic between them develop, a routine, approach her gently before inflicting the hurt.

Nothing in his life had been easier than taking Rose. No woman, among those he'd loved, had made his courtship so simple. Early on Rose understood that Charles was the leader with women, the one who placed limits, who structured unions through his control, his emotional strategy, through his reasonable practices of love. He led not by desire but tepidness, taking the moderate role, choosing to dam the torrent that emanated from women. The little animal that Rose was who loved with all of her heart often felt constrained, as if forced to move around in a wheelchair, but she didn't have the strength to leave it. In this story she had to conform, agree to his limits and renounce the love she expected from him, out of love for him.

After two years of living together, Charles' love hadn't moved an inch, still lukewarm, with no outpourings, a constant, a simple emotion that avoided disagreements and guaranteed the peace. Rose could acclimatize herself to this stable sort of love, the kind you find among cousins of the same family, but she couldn't ignore the fact that his desire for her had slowly fallen into slumber, after hitting a peak never since reached. His desire had lessened like every other desire in the world, by the simple fact of always having to see the same thing, the same scenery, for Charles the same small body, lips and tits that, over the years, had sagged a little, drooped, become flexible, like the norm, like nature—if by nature we mean what fades into the background, what doesn't break the continuity of shapes, colours, and tastes that have already been experienced, and anticipated, in this life.

Rose sometimes worried about this but hadn't begrudged him the change, since she herself did not have much desire for sex, an activity that was always portrayed as such a big thing, but that she could experience only from the outside, an actor playing a part. Even during Charles' greatest devotions, she always felt like she had no ability to arouse. For her, all erections were enshrouded in doubt, like an imposture, they couldn't really be meant for her, they had to have some secret quest for something she didn't possess.

Charles returned to his bachelor habits. She knew that after he worked on selecting and retouching photographs in his studio, he spent time on the Internet looking for those body parts that took his breath away, and forced him to gasp for air. She knew he was looking for parts of women he could drag his cursor over and enlarge, then bring his tongue to the screen as if to graze on the fetishistic morsels that made him lose his mind.

He didn't have to look for long. Thousands of websites, most of them sadomasochistic, were a real gold mine. The breasts and lips had almost always been operated on, alluding to human intervention, showing signs of mistreatment, voluntary bruising. When Rose was alone in the studio, she'd go through Charles' computer to find the images that often came in the form of short video clips he'd saved, always similar, like sisters. These segments of bodies troubled her by their strangeness and reminded her sometimes of the medical dictionary in her parents' house that had so impressed her as a child, a large red and white book her father liked to flip through.

To Rose's eyes, the images differed from the dictionary pictures only by their gaudy underwear, leather, latex, wigs, and makeup that showcased the particular body part. Lips came without a face, breasts without arms, asses without legs. A lot of images didn't represent sexually charged regions, but only bruises, blue on white skin, fragility exposing its true colours, scars, uneven parts not attached to pleasure.

But she knew nothing of how Charles quickly grew bored with his own weaknesses. She didn't know that the images he collected had a short lifespan that varied little from one picture to the next, their effect never felt beyond these first few days, she certainly didn't know he always felt sullied by jacking off and that his desire would return, a harassment, always the same. She had no idea that he hated the way the images, so irresistible at first, quickly became obsolete, he disliked the hunt for new ones, a pursuit renewed by his desire that didn't subside, though it would surely diminish with age but, for now, it made him track down his nourishment any way he could.

Once Charles had freed himself from his demons, the images packed on his screen were perceived in a different light, they took on another dimension, the invitation was transformed into an eviction: the nearly identical shapes, the parts of women he chose for their discordance, left him with an after-taste of shit, the feeling that all these pieces of meat would come alive, as they did when he was young, and demand justice from him. He realized that the butchery hadn't left him—far from it—it had just opened a new shop in the bodies of the women who got him hard. Sometimes horror would overtake him as he gazed at these headless women, detached, wounded, soulless, then he returned home to seek shelter in Rose's arms, consolation in her servitude as in a blanket, a comforter wrapped around his day, his shame.

ROSE WAS ON COLONIAL AVENUE, not far from her building. The scenery had begun reflecting her life again, the mass of passersby dominated by women. Rose had taken her surgical mask off and placed it in her handbag, raised the collar of the blouse she'd chosen for just that purpose since it covered her mouth, then she paid the driver and exited the cab.

The entrance to her building and the hallways were deserted, but the door to Julie's loft was ajar as if she was expecting someone, or hadn't closed it properly or, worse still, she wanted to be seen by her neighbours. This was exactly what Rose thought as she felt the dagger graze her neck again. Turning her key carefully to avoid the humiliation of being discovered hiding her mouth with her blouse, Rose overheard Julie speaking to someone, on the phone she guessed, a few words concerning the charms of a man she was extolling, a cascade of words crisscrossed with laughter, the flirtatious emotional connection before love emerged.

Before the mirror framed in Mexican pine, hanging in the entrance, Rose pulled her collar down, revealing her outsized lips like two pieces of meat that would drive Charles wild, at least for a couple of ejaculations.

She lay down on the bed, her veins still rushing with morphine; she wanted nothing more than to be there, lying on her back under the covers. She wanted to sink into the softness injected into her, the softest she'd ever felt, thank you, Dr. Gagnon, for upping the dose, she thought as she held a wet cloth filled with ice cubes to the swelling. Charles called to say that the shoot with an actress, a woman first seen in a movie where she played an exotic dancer, would go on late into the night, but knowing that Julie O'Brien couldn't possibly be with him, she didn't care.

It wasn't up to her to discover the truth of Charles' past, but she was bothered by how slow she was to get things through her mind, as her mother Rosine had told her over and over again, a woman who'd strung together one pregnancy after another, desperate to squeeze something else out of her womb besides girls.

Rosine was a loving mother, but truly miserable. She'd eventually set her heart on Rose after abandoning her for a year, maybe as a way of redeeming her mistake. She made Rose into a double of herself, showing her the path to fashion by teaching her to sew, the rudiments of the profession. Rose was close to her mother through her name but also her body. Like her mother, she was shaped like a pear, short and with no chest, narrow shoulders and large hips, a pear she managed to hide by sheer force of will, but that required no more than a moment of laziness to re-emerge, ripen, boil to the surface, she knew that to counter her natural shape she needed to stay vigilant by regimenting her food, then turning to surgery and exercise, avoiding pregnancy. Such was the advice offered in a convoluted way by fashion magazines on page after page but always between the lines. Rosine infiltrated her name and her genes, a mirror aimed at her, a graft that pulled her down.

Rose didn't want to be slow to get things through her mind, she hadn't seen her father's homosexuality, though he'd gotten his wife pregnant, his erections moved in an opposite direction from his mother, but had stayed long enough in her mother's pussy to spread his seed and reach her eggs. She loved her father endlessly, he couldn't be different from other men because he was the Norm, his tastes and manners, his reflections and ideas about the world, were magnified in Rose's eyes and took on the size of the universe, he could do no wrong and no harm, beyond reproach like every father in the world in their little girls' heart.

Her father's name was Renald Dubois and he came from Arvida, a small town that later would become Jonquières, not far from Chicoutimi where his father and grandfather were born. Beyond his grandfather he didn't know, he'd lost track of his ancestors, something he didn't care about. What mattered to him was never to reproduce there, to go as far as possible from the aluminum smelters where the men of his family had sacrificed their lives in heavy labour, all back and no brains, they'd laid down their lives in acid emissions, toxic dust in the air and the water, then died from a skewer of cancers: of the lungs and of the bladder, with intestinal diseases to boot.

For Rose, Renald Dubois had been the greatest, the strongest of fathers, far more than for her sisters, for whom only her mother was important. Her sisters had remained close as they got older, still more or less living as a family, without Rose who couldn't handle the oppression of her clan. Her only link to her family was the time spent during the holidays, and even then, she hadn't seen anyone in over two years, not even her mother.

Renald had met Rosine in high school in Chicoutimi, and produced his children one after another, mixing in a few encounters with men, always secret, underground, exhilarating. In the last years of his life, Rose found the courage to ask him questions, and the answers were a slap in the face and a door slammed shut: why had he married a woman, and how could he have had children with her?

"When you're like me, you have to have children young. Because after a certain age, it just doesn't work with women anymore. You've got to have them when a stiff breeze is enough to get you hard."

From deep in her bed, Rose recalled her father's words that must have had consequences for her, maybe even devastating, who knows, but she preferred to slip into sleep, far from him and the rest of the family.

A BLUE SKY above them. Rose watching Julie sitting in front of her at the neon orange picnic table, slut orange, Rose thought, slut like a bitch, a bitch like Julie. Out of the corner of her eye, she was itemizing Julie who was looking at her glass, seemingly discouraged, as if it was giving her reason to worry, as if it was a chalice before which she had to weigh the pros and cons, liquid torment on a summer's day.

They were on the roof of the building, affected by the heat, already slightly drunk on the white wine they'd just opened. The sky was blue and immense, a field open to change and transformation, from clouds forming at breakneck speed, accidents of the weather that could drown you in torrential rain at a moment's notice and, why not, another bolt of lightning, a *coup de grâce*, on the disembowelled guardrail, that visible injury that reminded Rose and Julie they were enemies and not friends, God saw them together on the roof and it was an outrage to His eyes.

The movement of the world is kneading, tearing apart. Life as lived from within is fated to be twisted under its own weight and bleed, Rose told herself, her head still full of that image of the lightning on the guardrail, and the shoes flying down below, expensive slippers she'd found the next day in the middle of Colonial Avenue, crushed by car wheels.

Rose had to find a way to return to her theory of the overabundance of women, her demographic theory of unhappiness that she'd always kept to herself, knowing deep down that she was exaggerating to impress. At one point, she reached into her handbag and took out a pack of cigarettes she'd bought for Julie an hour before, cigarettes for girls, baby girls, she'd mocked as she paid the Vietnamese corner store owner who never gave you a receipt for anything—fake cigarettes, long and ultralight, golden, with so little taste they were nothing at all, an impression of cigarettes, an empty movement of the hand toward the lips. Julie was shaken by that golden pack on the orange table, Rose noticed and relished it. But Julie's green eyes were magnets that she couldn't tear herself away from, and that changed things because she could see trouble brewing in those eyes, trouble only deepened that green, a vertigo green, eyes like an abyss. Rose hated her so much she had difficulty breathing, but at the same time she wanted to conquer her, stow her in her pocket to make sure she could keep Charles through the pact of friendship, but screw it, bullshit, Rose decided, screw the pact, screw this whole fucking story.

Rose woke up that morning to lips that weren't swollen at all, a new speed record, she'd worried about Charles being disappointed, how he'd lose his passion and might not want to touch her anymore. She'd undergone this operation a number of times always with the same results, but this time it was different, done with even greater skill than usual. Her lips were as spectacular as Julie's eyes. If her lips and those eyes existed on the same face, the world would be lost, forced to its knees. No mouth in the world could be more perfect, more inviting, in that morning light her lips were as she'd always wanted them, but she knew this state wouldn't last, her mouth would change like Dr. Gagnon always warned her when she asked about their life span. She knew she would atrophy, her mouth would move toward the thin line she'd first had as a mouth, if you could call it that, a gash forced on her by her mother Rosine, the opposite of carnal, an abhorrence.

Rose watched Julie. Julie smoked, her face dark with torment in front of her glass of white wine. Julie and her magnetic eyes, a redhead's green, her hair short and platinum, silvery reflections, Julie and her firm body, the four inches she had on her, Julie and her words, her turns of phrase, her manner above everyone else, her armour. This woman is fighting against something, alcohol maybe, Rose understood, remembering Bertrand's story about her, weeks before, on the Plan B patio. A woman fighting the desire to destroy herself, she'd thought, to lead her body to its death, where her soul lay already.

"Who fixed your lips?"

Rose wasn't expecting the question. She felt betrayed, outplayed. What she was hoping would be sublime had led to her fall; she'd been unmasked. The perfection seen in the mirror was revealed to be no more than the place of her origins, the zero degree of past time, Rosine's gash, her father's wrong gender, her lips, freshly emerged from their swelling, now disclosed what was underneath them, her beauty was a finger pointed at the disgrace she had attempted to correct. Then Julie moved onto her breasts, arrogance over arrogance, cutting, sadistic.

"I don't know who did your breasts, but I'm sure it's the same person who did your lips. Your body has a signature, the work comes from the same hand. It shows."

Of course, everything could be seen, that was the great paradox of female vanity, the disguise, always the same, mass-marketed and purchased by women who then sold themselves to men, to buy new bodies that made men get harder. What else could she expect?

Up on the roof, what occurred next was hazy. She had the vague sensation of the sky moving, its threat above her, it accompanied her theory about women and a dramatic aggregation of clouds, growing with the same intensity as her speech, painting the sky with fury. For the rest of her life she would remember her tirade as something that swept her away as she dropped the pieces she wanted to keep, to have mastered the situation with statistics that didn't seem to interest Julie, but that revealed instead another scar entirely, the sickness of being one too many among others, her pussy that inspired no passion, rejected by her father and avoided by Charles who preferred the rest.

They left for Plan B, falling headfirst into Rose's world, splayed out before them, populated with women. The vision of the patio and the inside of the bar threw Julie into a trance, as if she were opening her eyes for the first time, harassing the women in the bar with questions: where were they from, where were they going, what should we do now? They ate, talked, and confided in alcohol. Julie revealed everything, or so it seemed to her, about Steve, and the inconsolable grief that had killed her. At one point Julie took Rose by the hand and kissed her, a warm new sensation for Rose who was kissing a woman for the first time in her life. It was a sexless kiss, sisters of the mouth, a symbol of two tongues touching to show the people around them that sisterhood wasn't just some vain wish, it wasn't an urban legend, it existed, true enough, through sexual exhibition in bars to get folks talking. Rose felt seduced by Julie who was seduced herself, and for a few hours her predictions seemed ridiculous and over-the-top, at least until Charles showed up at the Tap Room, where Rose's restlessness—exacerbated by cocaine— forced her back to the predictions that were materializing faster and faster as the night wore on. Bertrand felt her disintegrating and tried to piece her back together with reassurance. Bertrand and his scraggly body, his wiry hair, his extravagant shirts covered in colours, Hawaiian flowers. Bertrand unsuccessfully tried to woo Julie, so he hated her too.

"It's just the drugs, Rose," he said. "Coke makes you talk and forget the world. Nothing exists except what you have to say. Anybody will do as a listener."

"I know, but it's more than that. It's stronger than that. It was there before tonight. I've felt it for a long time. From the start."

Bertrand lit a cigarette then lit one Rose had been holding for some time now, letting Charles and Julie move off, walking fast, talking, on Mount Royal Avenue, toward their building.

"Real feelings can't resist cocaine," he went on. "The drug eats them. When you're high they fade away, but they come back the next day, and stronger than before because you'd lost them. You get attached to what disappeared, because it isn't normal, that feelings disappear like that. The next day you're scared. It's the drugs, Rose."

But Rose was pulling away from the world, far from the couple, Charles and Julie, who were talking to forget her as she retreated, the witness to other couples, as she'd always been.

Making a scandal was beyond Rose. When she contemplated other people's pleasure, she could be at best reverent, like during the photo shoots, and at worst petrified, like that night. She and Bertrand didn't want to follow Charles to Julie's loft, knowing how much the two had to say to each other.

"Don't worry, Rose. You can't fuck on cocaine, not when you don't know the other person. Getting a hard-on is too much work, especially when you throw in alcohol. It takes way too much time. Let's leave them alone and have our own little party, just you and me, at your place."

They went to Rose's place, and Bertrand had started reminiscing about their time together, their trip to Mexico and their trip to Las Vegas where they almost married. A few hours went by, and Rose couldn't think of anything but what might be happening on the other side of the hall. She imagined them talking, smoking, and drinking, but from between their words she could see Charles' cock, the tip of it pointing at Julie's breasts with their hard nipples, his tongue. Through Bertrand's monologue she contemplated pornographic images of the contained attraction between two people, an attraction made of the stuff of destiny that finally gave way to flesh. Once Bertrand left, Rose understood she wouldn't be able to sleep. She knew she would see these images, she pictured them already, it was her duty to see them.

Rose walked out the door and spent several minutes in the hall between the two apartments, standing in front of the unlocked door. Even before she went inside, she knew they weren't talking, they were already in bed. Charles and the noises he made guided her toward them, a ghost slipping into their intimacy, hugging the walls, making herself as small as possible, she who was too small as it was. Julie was giving herself, her eyes closed, on her back, her T-shirt above her breasts, as if absent, beautiful in her unconsciousness, while Charles masturbated with an intensity Rose hadn't witnessed since their early days together, he took his hand from his cock for a moment to touch Julie's breasts, then he grabbed it again and went at himself more furiously, making sounds that froze her to the spot, and that she would remember the rest of her life: Charles making sounds with his mouth but not for her, his hand coming and going over his cock but not for her, Charles and his panting noises like chains that bound her to Julie's bed without her being invited into it, chains that bound her to what was happening between them that made them forget her, Julie unconscious and offering her body as she lay on her back and Charles keeping himself on the threshold of himself, about to explode, postponing ejaculation out of the pleasure of Julie's breasts.

Then at some point, Charles saw Rose and hesitated, his cock at the max, electric. He'd gone too far to consider her but not to consider her made it impossible for him to continue, at least not with any peace of mind. They made eye contact and it lasted painfully long, as if he was waiting for her consent to keep going, and Rose had to flee, knowing Julie had seen her, since she sat up in bed because she must have felt that Charles had stopped, she wore an expression of innocence, at a loss.

Back home, Rose dialled Dr. Gagnon's emergency number in a panic, it was his home number, it was the middle of the night, she didn't know if he had a wife, or anything else about him, praying to God for him to answer and come and take her away, far from here, far from this place where she was disappearing from the world.

VI

ALL CATS ARE GREY

JULIE O'BRIEN WAS running on the treadmill at Nautilus. She was Nelly Furtado. She was feeling good, finally, she could hurt herself without shrinking, and listen to pop music at full volume, she was the Star, the woman who bewitches every man, a crowd of men who dream of nothing else but sticking their cocks in her. Her desire for sex was gone, but she retained the idea of attraction, she understood that sex was at the centre of all beings, the heart of all ambition. The women who faced the stage all dreamed of being her, with her pussy desired by all, a black hole, singing and dancing and doing everything effortlessly. The greatest pleasure of existence is to be idolized, sucking up people's attention as you keep them at a distance, filling yourself with people without choosing them, taking their love and not giving anything back.

The sweat that covered her body like a shroud exhaled the poisons, she thought, it breathed out the shit she'd been wallowing in for five days, it had been her life for years, shit that was a nest for vermin, the vermin of her cheap period, she thought, looking around, a period of screens, Botox, self-love, and invincibility, the Madonna period.

Facing Julie who was Nelly Furtado were ten television screens, five of which showed people training with a smile and without a drop of sweat. They were tanned orange and ran as they made comments, with painted smiles, you could buy the machine that was making them run, so said the banner, in ten easy payments, and Julie imagined that machine in her loft, impossible to resist, in her mind she moved it to see if there was enough room. Some thirty members of the gym were running in front of those ten screens, five of which displayed information about physical exercise, which was all about how you felt inside, the soul, the screens claimed, wellness, self-esteem, orderly and healthy thoughts, welcome and positive like fridge magnets. On the other screens MuchMusic played, young naked women dancing without a care for each other, one next to the other, showing off their asses jiggling to the beat, hostile solitudes surrounding one man, the Leader of the Horde, the hip-hop singer, covered in gold, surrounded by undulating hips that opened up to pussy, holes that had never had children. Then Oprah, obese women, the tears of women who would never dance around a hip-hop artist, never be invited to faceoff against each other with their pussies, women who offered themselves up, but in vain. Then the ads, skin and bodies before and after, acne be gone, lines on faces now unlined, inverted countdowns to smaller waist sizes, skinnier than teenagers. Then CNN, the rumble of war, counting up the dead, the anonymous tide of veiled women, neither friend nor foe, neither submissive nor revolutionary, just veiled, CNN and CBC, the major news networks, were the other side of the story, the opposite and inverse face of the exercise rooms built for the viability and impermeability of bodies, machines designed to prevent the spillage of vital organs in trenches, the leaking of the self out of the self, in battle.

Julie wasn't watching the screens, she was a Star, she was watching herself on a stage around which she imagined a crowd, screaming and begging for her, see me, see me so I might love myself. She felt pathetic, she knew she was ridiculous. Tics of satisfaction flashed over her face, other gym members saw them and took them as signs of insanity, the proof that something wasn't right, bats in her belfry about to take flight, haze in her mind that blurred her. But once again it was stronger than she was, the omniscient existence of God was just out of her grasp. It was like Marilyn Monroe's desire to die that she'd read about in a book, that had her crying over passages where she was described as halfway dead already, a zombie. To be nothing and the fear that comes from that possibility—that was unbearable beyond not being fuckable anymore—the book about Marilyn revealed a truth: to be nothing is worse than being dead. Julie had understood through Marilyn.

She kept running in front of the screens that made people run. She wondered if religion's first function was to make sin the building block of men so they might attempt to turn their ego into a holy thing, and finally release it, abandon their ego so great, so overbearing, a face hungry for attention, devourer of others, a giant despot. These days everyone was their own star and there was no more audience. God had died and kept his creatures from loving anything else but themselves, his creatures were forced to find truth in mental and physical health, and structure their lives around hygiene. The empty space where God had been was replaced by a billion trinkets, and now people were running on machines toward control, stability, and the celebration of their bodies, toward their eternity, perpetual brilliance.

Julie was still Nelly Furtado. But there was something different in her usual thoughts, always the same, about the ways existence found to perpetuate itself. The crowd that was watching her sing "Maneater" had a new onlooker: Charles. He was part of the crowd, watching her too, at first an invader, he'd become the Eye whose gaze embodied all others, he was the Eye through which she was beheld. Julie felt herself in love, as close to happiness as a woman like her could be. Charles alone was reason enough to make her run on her machine, toward his eyes, and he was her neighbour in real life. She asked herself that question that only women about to fall in love ask themselves: what if he isn't into me? And then: what if I was naturally vulgar, and my vulgarity like a howl among wolves? Yet this morning, under her door, she'd found a note written on a lined sheet of white paper, folded in half:

Julie,

I really enjoyed our evening. Even if it was weird, it was good. We should see each other again to talk about the documentary and, why not, life. Rose and I have separated. Not because of you, it's just life. I think she's doing well. She went to live somewhere else but she comes and goes, she has the keys. We have to be discreet, so write me a note and put it behind the newspaper rack, in the entrance.

Charles

The note reassured her. She immediately wrote to tell him he was welcome at her place. There was a secret way up: take the elevator down to the entrance then climb back up to the third floor via the fire escape that led to her back door which she would leave open. He could come to her place without being seen and he could go back the way he came.

Her sixty minutes of cardio were done. The Star left the stage the moment Julie took her earphones off. Without music the pleasure of being a star lost much of its intensity, the performance was cancelled and Julie fell back to earth, into a reality where she wasn't sure she actually was anyone at all.

She continued her workout as she had a hundred times before, concentrating on her back and biceps that day. She would lie on her back, a bar in her hands extended over her head, sometimes on all fours, a weight in one hand, sometimes sitting at different angles, a weight in each hand. She concentrated on the movements that warmed her body and made her cry out softly, groans that brought sex to mind, sex that had disappeared from her life but might, with Charles, who knows, be given new life.

Often her cries of pain attracted men's attention, they themselves were grunting, but louder, so many ephemeral trophies of athletic success, cries that proved they had pushed themselves to their limit, given their all. Sometimes the sounds were like what Julie imagined orgies would be for blind people: moving bodies occupying a given space, hitting each other, seeking pleasure that involuntarily expressed itself with breath, from the nose and mouth, leaks from inside out like secrets impossible to keep. When she closed her eyes, the whole room became an orgy of solitudes busy in front of the mirrored walls, not touching each other, looking at each other but pretending not to, through the mirrors, their grunts intertwined, a thick mixture of sound droppings, smells and sweat, quick glances out of the corners of eyes, sometimes mutual, given and received in the mirrors that multiplied bodies in their orgy.

Julie lived in gyms the way she lived at home; she exercised the way she put on her slippers; she worked her muscles the way she watched television. She couldn't live without this way of moving, sweating, filling a part of every day with mechanical effort that didn't require thought. She couldn't live without this burning in her flesh that enveloped her, calmed her, real inner peace for hours that consisted of a straight line of emotions, armour against negative thoughts. A stable warmth without flare-ups or cool-offs, and when she found herself away from the gym for too long, she could feel herself slipping through her own fingers, falling into approximation, her ideas would begin to lose shape and come together in a single mass and Julie would get that feeling of leaking out of herself, like a snowman in the rain, shredded by the wind. She knew the price to pay for rebuilding herself with mistreatment when she was broken, and the price was restrictive; she couldn't risk losing what had made her a statue, made her stone.

At thirty-three, Julie couldn't travel anymore or seek new adventures with a pack on her back, destination of new worlds and cultures; the unpredictable was not a possibility for her. She could not, except rarely, sleep in a bed that wasn't hers, skip a meal or change her diet that suited her training. Her youth was done. She'd mistreated herself so much that she couldn't take pleasure from being somewhere foreign, unless she had the means to recreate what she'd left behind, a way of controlling her work schedule, her meals, her food, and her sleep, unless she could be anywhere in the world the way she was at home.

She recently refused the opportunity to shoot a movie in Europe, hating herself for it, a film where she would have interviewed collectors of World War II detritus. She was supposed to interview and write a script based on the stories of these collectors who were also diggers in the earth, who searched for all sorts of objects, pieces of planes, weapons, ammunition, and other materials of war, not to mention human remains, then exhibited them in museums that people would pay to visit, museums these collectors set up in their own houses in the German, Belgian, Polish, and French countryside. In the detritus they sometimes found skulls, femurs, and thoraxes with shreds of clothes on them. Most of these collectors were nutty, which should have made the project interesting, given her the desire to move forward with it, but she'd refused, unable to imagine working blindly in the far-flung countryside, away from big cities, and worse, the work would have put her into contact with the remains of existences long gone; she'd have to spend time with dead things that had been pieces of another dead thing; a plane, a tank or, worse, a human body. It wasn't the theme itself that terrified her but the way she would have to encounter it, through dispersion and dissipation—who knows whether after a few weeks there'd be any difference between her and the unearthed remains, who could tell whether, in the end, she'd get comfortable in these cemeteries, and begin to rot for good.

Nautilus was full of men. Julie pushed herself hard, she was exhausted but couldn't stop. Like a lot of people she believed in going beyond her limits, reaching perfection through abuse. To respond to her recent excesses and go as far in her workout as she had in the bars, she added extra weight for each exercise, overestimating her strength and endurance. While executing the "Arnold Press," a complex movement invented by Arnold Schwarzenegger himself, her left arm, the weaker of the two, couldn't sustain the extra pressure, and at the fifth repetition her wrist bent backward.

A sharp and blinding pain exploded in her muscle, a stab, a

white thunderbolt in her shoulder but also in her head, the lightning made her howl in the middle of the busy herd. The intense pain forced her eyes shut as if her vision, usually turned outward, had retreated to attend to the pain that bent her in two, made her fall on her knees, holding her left elbow with all the strength of her right hand and bringing her head as close as possible to her shoulder, her eyes still shut, concentrating on the only thing that mattered: the fire that rose from her injury.

She left the gym in an ambulance and in absolute confusion, whisked off to the Hôtel-Dieu emergency room where she got a dose of morphine, quickly followed by another after the doctor realized the first was having little effect, something Julie proved by her constant groaning and by the fact that she was turned into herself, absent to the world. She was sent home, her shoulder and left arm in a sling after an X-ray showed that despite the shock, there was no dislocation.

e'd have to stay away from ld be a matter of months, e could scarcely measure, ure was compromised but ting and understanding she come a statue. On the con- through the enjoyment of lterated, from the medicine escription for Empracet that p her warm, and never to be mixed with alcohol.

At home, she found a second note from Charles under her door, an answer to hers.

Julie,

Tonight, 7:00, at your place. Can't wait. Leave your door open. Leave a message downstairs if you can't.

Charles

IT WAS TOO LATE, almost midnight and Julie, her shoulder in a sling, couldn't figure out what to do. She wanted to sleep right now, but also wanted to take time to write to Charles with her good hand. He must have found a locked door closed and been unhappy not to find a message explaining what had happened, but he couldn't wait and that's what counted, oh God, let his excitement last, let him be patient, she hoped, make sure my shoulder doesn't come between us, like Rose. Before going to bed she wrote a note and set it downstairs behind the newspaper rack, the story of her accident and the emergency room that offered, in closing, her sincere apologies followed with a heartfelt kiss. They could see each other tomorrow night at her place if he could be there, she swore.

THE MONTHS THAT followed were troubling and filled with pleasure, at least that's how Julie O'Brien would remember it. The strangest part was that once their story began, she didn't have much to say about it, maybe because the joys of love can't be understood through words that never reflect true emotion, unless they're kept close to the heart, words can't come close to describing them, in the end, words serve only to give yourself a second chance to love lost things.

Charles Nadeau's love rebuilt Julie's capacity to love. She'd been exhumed and brought back to life. Love at first sight, she'd thought for a time, blind, mutual love, steamy love that rises in a wave from her guts to her face, joining the weather, the sun's daggers on her fair, russet skin, so poorly adapted to climate change, a movement toward the spread of the desert across the globe, and the demonization of good weather. Love had broken the weight of the world that oppressed her and forced her into her loft, filled with cushions, sleepy cats, and drawn blinds.

She wouldn't find much to say about this love, except that her life felt lighter. Something of the aridity of the world had lessened, relaxed, become less tense, the world had stopped fighting against itself, a strange and surprising magic that softened its surface, as if love could straighten the order of things, giving them logic, filling them with necessity. For a while she could say that God had hidden his plan well and that the Devil could crawl back to Hell. The universe was forgiven, it had been right to give birth and make the chaos in her heart flourish. The universe had a key that Julie finally held in her hand: life came from death only to meet love, before returning to death, this is what she understood. It was as simple as that, there was no reason to make it complicated.

The summer of love continued in its fullness, then turned to autumn that would soon arrive, a magnificent season with the return of a more reasonable sun, less biting, a sun that invested, as time passed, an orbit further from Earth, giving more room for autumn to advance, and proclaim itself the most beautiful period of the year, still warm but not hot, with drier air flowing more freely. Filled with affection and new understanding, she contemplated the thousands parading down Saint Denis Street protesting Israel's invasion of Lebanon. The Israeli army had entered Lebanon to dismantle Hezbollah, and the Lebanese, with this invasion, were thrown back into their past, into the horrors of the civil war and the scars it left behind. The scars were palpable beneath the reconstruction, in the modern architecture. What had been bombed was bombed again, rubble lay underneath the solid surface of Lebanon, roads and buildings ready to crumble again, and fall apart with the smallest shake, so that the loss of life, of children and friends, could begin again and again, counting the dead, the impossible grief of armed vengeance, mourning, without end, in the hatred of your neighbour, the ultimate goal of your life.

People around the world had risen in protest, among them Jews, following the path of the march, sticking out from the others in their fur hats and long black coats to their feet in the blazing sun. A human tide had walked for hours on Saint Denis Street as Julie smiled upon them because she was in love, she would have taken anybody's side under any pretext because she thought she was in love, she wanted to be with them, out in the world, and not by herself, in her shelter, because she thought she was in love. Love had brought her back to the world, where everything had its place.

She wasn't working out anymore and that didn't bother her, another miracle of love. She'd been afraid her body would disintegrate but it didn't happen, and wouldn't as long as she could walk and even run, as long as her shoulder remained in place, fixed and stable in its sling. The wars of the world and the rainstorms over Montreal could do all they wanted, as long as she could be with Charles in some café over lunch and at night at her place, with or without alcohol.

Love had blinded her for a time to Charles' warped tastes, his tics and obsessions that didn't bother her, at least not at first, probably because she couldn't see how deep they were. Months passed before this crease in the bed, that she called all sorts of names, eventually pulled them apart by creating a tribunal for Charles that would shower him with accusations, and weigh him down with judgements.

In the evening they would more often than not be at her place, whether Rose was in the apartment on the other side of the hall or not. Julie knew very little about Rose since she'd separated from Charles, two or three things, such as her finding refuge in the home of a man whose identity remained secret. That's all Julie wanted to know: let Rose not be alone, let her be well-protected, but far away from them. She wished her well but she wished it to happen elsewhere, she wanted her happy life to reach her from a great distance, like a postcard dropped in her mailbox, from some beach down South, written by a cousin whose name she'd forgotten.

Charles had irregular hours, and he could arrive at any time between six and 9:00 PM. He walked into her house without knocking and on tiptoe, always a little late, as if it was nothing, surprising her sometimes as she was waiting in the middle of the living room, cigarette in hand, with a strong desire for alcohol, on sale everywhere, so many opportunities to come back to earth, to return to sleep.

Every time he walked into her loft, he would greet her the same way. "Hey, there, backy-back!"

He gave her that nickname the night of the now-famous bacchanal, an "anal night," she had called it, her attempt to say it would join the annals of history. All night he'd called her "backy-back," two words joined by a hyphen, exotic and playful. The first night it bothered her, but once she was in love, she welcomed with open arms the dose of affection contained in the name he'd given her, as silly as it was.

When Charles had come in this way on one of their first nights together, she didn't smile, unhappy about his lateness, as slight as it was.

"I thought you weren't coming. I was about to go out," she'd lied.

"Sorry, I did my best," he answered, offering up a liquor store bag with two bottles of white wine.

More of that damned Chardonnay, Julie thought, for once she couldn't care less about the bottles and the oblivion they promised. She maintained her sullen silence, unable to hide the girlish pout of someone waiting for an apology. Her grumpy air softened Charles.

"Lately, I've been working with actresses and singers with no experience. It takes longer, plus I have to train a new stylist. It's hard working with a new girl. It takes time to create the chemistry, and communicate without always having to talk. It isn't as fluid as before. But it doesn't matter, that's just the way it is."

Charles was attracted by Julie's shoulder in its sling revealed by her transparent blouse, and he touched her, softly at first, laying his hand on her, then more firmly, gripping and releasing, gripping again, like a cat pawing the ground where he intends to sleep, preparing his territory.

"Hey! Careful!" Julie exclaimed as Charles' eyes began to glaze over. "It's still fresh!"

Charles released his grip, though he left his hand on her shoulder, a hand as wide as a racket, long, eager fingers, the way she liked them.

"I've been thinking of you all day," he confessed, taking his hand away as if he were sorry to. "It's hard to think of one woman when you're trying to photograph another. I could barely get the focus. I don't have to go back until tomorrow afternoon, so we can go crazy tonight, if you like."

"We'll have to go crazy in my little loft," Julie said, reaching for the bag to show she accepted his gift, his presence, his words, his paw on her.

They moved into the living room, sat down, and began talking, drinking wine in small mouthfuls, going back to Charles and his past again, his father's butcher shop, but also other things, a conversation made of small sounds that served to narrow the distance between two people interested in each other, to unite them, chit-chat as the pretext to breathing in the other person's scent.

And love, miracle of miracles, removed alcohol's malevolent power. Its call had stopped torturing Julie, or not as much as before. She wouldn't lose herself entirely, and she knew why. It was Charles. Charles as a resting place, a safety net. She wouldn't fall into shamelessness with him a second time, she wouldn't let her vulgarity sully everything, especially since she was on medication and the softness of her loft didn't inspire excess, it was like a lullaby, a feather bed, an endless candlelight evening, a hearth fire burning for hours on end that flowed without discord.

While talking about nothing in particular, Julie realized, for the first time, that Charles was beautiful, despite the fact that he was often around. Men's beauty, she noticed, didn't come at you head-on, you had to discover it slowly, over time, like a soul, or a temperament. It was different from women's beauty, not made of artifice and constant efforts on the surface, but of flesh, the product of a father and mother in their depth, it could be groomed but was not a product of grooming, it had nothing to do with the beauty of women, aggressive, jumping out at you, made of successive applications of layers on the skin that compelled your attention like a fire alarm. This beauty that existed without special measures was durable, it didn't age ungracefully like women. The different illumination of the sexes, Julie observed, was the worst injustice because it made the path of women infinitely more brutal and difficult, they who lived in a constant stream of light like an interrogation, a search, an examination that covered them from head to toe, turned them into asses, complete pussies.

But all that would change, Julie predicted, she was attentive to the transformations of the era, everyone would end up equal, and just as brutal. Men's bodies, even homosexuals, would begin to feminize and be forced to follow the imperatives of beauty, the requirements, the commandments, men would have to own the same products as women but masked with different colours, red, brown, green, deep blue, grey, and black. The difference between men and women would be reduced to the wrapping of their respective beauty products, and who knows, maybe men's cocks would stop getting hard to imitate women and turn toward their own image, captivated by the mirror, revealed and hidden by the illusionist's vicious burqa, the disguise whose cost is so dear.

Charles was much more beautiful than Steve, though they shared a number of features, their similarity bothered Julie because it pointed to a continuity in her tastes. Charles was tall with blue eyes, salt and pepper hair, his eyebrows were very close together and they gave him a permanent look of concentration and intelligence, he had giant hands that manipulated her in bed and put her in her place, an attitude of immobility and attention, they directed her toward his favourite angles, the porn shots that innumerable men of his generation preferred, but she also took pleasure in them since she had a body for porn, she had a pornographic essence…like so many other women. Charles and Julie were of their time, they loved their neighbours with the means they had.

As well as his shining, lush hair, Charles had a full and sensual mouth, a mouth that Rose and Julie would have killed to have, the kind they were trying to draw on their faces with injection after injection. Charles looked like an angel, a Saint Francis of Assisi, he was so beautiful that he disturbed those who looked at him too closely, and once his beauty was seen, no one could miss it. That was what Julie believed that night, never thinking his beauty would destroy them by provoking her jealousy, or the beauty of his models, but the sex that lay behind it.

"You're beautiful," he told her that night as she was admiring his beauty.

After the collapse of moral and religious institutions, after the historical destruction of the notions of duty, sacrifice, self-abnegation—in short, established order—only beauty was left to join two beings, and money too, of course, that tends to accumulate around beautiful people. Socially, love was no longer the opposite of prostitution, and prostitution that sells people, selected the most beautiful, that was the Darwinian logic, the return to primitive behaviour, trophies for baboons. Despite love's mutation toward the most savage discrimination, Julie believed that love made fools of people, its voluptuous stultifying was a constant through the ages, and it gave the world its lightness.

That night she kept remembering Marilyn Monroe who, one sad day, had written or said these beautiful words: "When you love someone you give them the power to kill you." In any couple, there is always a killer and someone killable, the killer always kills despite himself, without wanting to and without pleasure. In a relationship the killable person always more or less gives herself up to the slaughter, often doing the job herself, and what the killable person can't stand is not to be killed, but to not inspire in the killer the desire to kill. So you have to bring the murder about yourself, thinking about the killer, the criminal who is absent from the scene of the crime.

But for now Charles liked her as much as she liked him, she was the Star on their private stage where they were enough for each other, far from the audience.

"What's that?" Charles asked, pointing at a large plant on a small Indian cabinet, with a single yellow fruit.

"A lemon. I've had this tree for almost a year, and it's produced just one lemon."

"Is that normal?"

"No idea. The tree didn't come with an instruction manual."

They contemplated the lemon for a while, for some time, as if they expected to see it fall, right there, at any moment, suddenly ill at ease in their silence at the centre of which hung a lemon without inspiring any thought in particular, a silence that announced a separation, or perhaps the opposite, their bodies coming together.

"When it falls, I'll let you know. We can make a fish dish with it, or cocktails," she breathed into Charles neck.

Invited by her breath, Charles kissed her impatiently, getting straight to the point, first nibbling at her lips, then lifting her shirt, opening it wide to see the sling around her painful shoulder that excited him so much, likely because Julie was suffering, moving his hands against her breasts, kneading them roughly, pinching her stiff nipples through the fabric of her bra. Then he climbed on top of her and freed her breasts from her bra, they were hard from the prosthesis, he pulled his jeans down and took out his cock. The way Charles acted reminded Julie of the forgotten movements of their last encounter, they were exactly the same, this repetition, she understood, is what gave shape to what had happened that night, to what had existed without being understood. Julie was a captive of Charles' determination, she felt an insistent and unexpected warmth between her legs, with one hand she grabbed Charles' cock and he came immediately, two thick squirts of semen aimed at her breasts landed on her chin, then ran down her neck.

That was it, it was over, it had lasted less than a minute and Julie was incredulous of how quickly his semen had spurted onto her, she was even more surprised by the heat she was feeling below, in her open casket, a bothersome sting that wouldn't quit, a need, like a fledgling opening its beak toward its mother's mouth.

Julie guided his hand toward her wet pussy, for that operation she had to take her panties off, get up and change position, with her above and him below. Charles began to stroke her but the time it took for that touch to reach her was too long. The heat had diminished, and though Charles tried to awaken it, the fire had gone out, maybe because he tried so hard, the red embers turned grey, all that remained was a feeling of cold annoyance as he obstinately worked on her. He had lost his erection, and there was no sense to it.

But Charles wasn't done yet. They fucked four times that night, on the couch and even on the floor, if you can call fucking the act of coming on her breasts and shoulder. Julie managed to come twice by touching herself, her two first times in years, another miracle, a resurrection in her existence where sex had become no more than a word, a concept, a zone hidden under the snow, the North Pole. Here was proof of her successful reintegration back to life, the dead matter of her body could still offer her that pleasure.

They ended up falling asleep together in Julie's big bed where her three Siamese cats joined them, and they woke up early the next morning and realized that the chemistry, the electric love, was still there. For the months that followed, they spent all their time together.

JULIE WAS IN a café, sitting at a table she had chosen years before, imposing her choice on the customers, settling down in such an everyday fashion that no one would have thought of disputing her right to that table. Always the same table in front of the large window that looked onto Saint Denis Street, at the Java U.

The café was small and not very busy, neither deserted nor packed, its advantage was that it was right next to her house. The café had become an extension of her living room, a house with changing décor, always a background to what she was writing on her computer, a white Macintosh that looked like a toy, a piece of candy. The decor included passersby and regular customers who also had their assigned table and whom she didn't talk to or barely, just to say a brief hello, barely lifting her head, the minimal movement that recognition required.

Java U had become her café by the simple fact that she frequented the place and had eased into it, she had been accepted as an obstinate regular, someone who tipped well and paid her bill. Her assiduity guaranteed the respect of the staff who kept the table for her with a small cardboard reservation sign until eleven, after which, if she hadn't yet arrived, they took the sign away with no hard feelings, preferring, however, when she called if her plans took her elsewhere on a given day. She even managed to get them to lower the volume of the music when she judged it too loud, or to change the music altogether when the same awful tune came on, most often techno that, she told them, was music strictly made for nights of dancing and drugs, and not for a morning of writing, not for the concentration that work required. She believed the music could change the taste of the coffee, giving it a hurried, upset flavour.

Julie was facing her laptop screen and typing willy-nilly ideas and impressions, early thoughts on her scenario. She was trying to structure it around Charles' personal story, but Rose's too, her ideas about her work, including her apocalyptic vision of female demography. She decided to include Rose in the script, this young woman who had magnificently disappeared from her relationship, a woman who'd abdicated without a fight, almost too good to be true. She had a plan in mind but hadn't yet mentioned it to Charles, as if she didn't want to put Rose back in the picture, at least not yet.

Julie believed that, with time, Rose would reveal herself to be like Justine in Marquis de Sade's *Justine or The Misfortunes of*

Virtue, still standing a virgin after the worst depravation. She believed that, by the time the script dragged through the procedural chain that led to actual filming, Rose would have gotten back on her feet and might laugh off everything that happened with the help of time and distance. She figured that Rose might still be in a relationship with her mystery man who saved her on that shipwrecked night and who, according to the little Charles knew, was rich.

"He has a lot of money." That was the only information Rose disclosed about her man, all she said to Charles when they spoke to each other over the phone or face to face, in her former loft when she sometimes came to grab a few boxes. She threw the other man's money in Charles' face like a reproach or a confession, as if money was the only thing this man possessed, as if this other man could only have value in something Charles didn't possess, or not very much of, because he couldn't give it to her in droves. Neither Charles nor Julie knew at the time that through this other man's talent, his skills as surgeon, Rose was plotting to win back Charles, or just destroy him.

Outside, winter was plastering its intense cold over the frozen city, held in sway, a cold that made everything crack under the ice, the roads that, come springtime, would expose thousands of potholes, deep holes that would damage thousands of cars. In the café the music was too loud, it made the place feel like a bar, it was so loud its presence became physical, it entered the body at chest level and turned them into beat boxes, but Julie didn't hear it, the bass was pushed to the limit but didn't make her resonate, the way the sun and the heat didn't lacerate her, or the cold burn her, the traffic noise had stopped oppressing her when she was stuck in a traffic jam.

A homeless man came into the café and was immediately shooed out by an employee, a cup of coffee was knocked over and fell to the floor, shattering. A surprised shriek from a customer who'd scalded herself penetrated the underlying noise of the music and flowed into it, the woman's shriek now part of the beat as if the music had been waiting for it to move forward, combining it into its rhythm. But Julie heard nothing of this noise, she was in love and her love was beginning to feel like a terrible blanket, love was beginning to bare its teeth and change into a snare, her love that only until recently had been an opening, a new way to see the world.

She was entirely concentrated on her script; she had become too close to it. She was working with impressions, visions in which people's souls materialized. In her memory she kept the image of Rose on the roof of the building, her head against the sky-blue background, anger growing inside her.

According to Rose, at birth there were 52% girls and 48% boys, while in reality, according to Quebec statistics she'd consulted on the Internet, it was the opposite. World-wide, there were 105 boys born for 100 girls, and Quebec was no exception: in 2001, 37,033 boys were born for 34,709 girls, and in 2003, 37,127 boys for 35,066 girls. That same year in Quebec, there were 190,048 boys aged 0 to 4 years for 179,590 girls. If women were more numerous than men on Earth, it was because mortality rates were higher for men at all ages, and if women were more numerous than men in Montreal, in particular in trendy neighbourhoods, it wasn't because they were born in greater numbers, but because they moved there in greater numbers. It was as simple as that. That was the difference Rose was talking about, and instead of being happy about this truth, she preferred to lie to stay within her kin, even outside her native Saguenay.

As for her calculations about homosexuals, they were unverifiable, since the definition of homosexuality itself was subjective, contrary to biological gender, which was clear: boy or girl, blue or pink, cock or pussy. On the Internet, the statistics weren't clear and left too much room for interpretations that could never be official. The rates varied between 8% and 20% of the population and, obeying society's obsession with equality, they forced society as a whole to be answerable to egalitarian values, and so the statistics made no distinction between the sexes, implicitly creating an equivalence of homosexuality rates between men and women.

But no matter. Rose's understanding of the world was out of sync with reality, forged from childhood trauma; the distance between truth and interpretation was what interested Julie more than the numbers themselves. Truth was no friend to numbers, it came from elsewhere, from the suffering of not being indispensable to the world, for example, what was the place from which all interpretations of the world emerged.

She was thinking these thoughts when Charles walked into the café and sat down, without being noticed, preferring to itemize her with a smile, taking his time.

"Hey, backy-back, I was looking for you. But I can't stay long."

Julie lifted her eyes to Charles in his white shirt with fine black lines, a Diesel. He looked like a photograph, with his face placed square in the middle. The café music had emerged at the same time he had, oppressive, noise pollution so early in the morning. Yet Charles had simply given birth to what was already there, on the cusp of her senses. Her world had been reduced to this, a certain light Charles cast around him in a circumference defined by his shadow that changed depending on the time of day, and he was always the centre of it.

"It's a coincidence. I need to talk to you."

She stood up to kiss him, pressing her lips against Charles' mouth and keeping them there a long time, looking for a touch of electricity, a shock.

"Rose needs to be a part of this documentary project. She might want to say what she thinks. That's just her style, right, to want to admire herself on the screen?"

As she spoke, something shimmered in Charles' eyes. With no apparent reason, like a reflex, he opened Julie's date book at a random page, something he never did, discovering two pages covered with his own first name written at every angle and in different colours: Charles in red, Charles in blue, Charles in pink, green, grey, black. Like a little girl, he thought, not without embarrassment, like a schoolgirl in puppy love, who wastes her time daydreaming and colouring.

"I don't think that's a good idea," he replied, looking at her date book, seeing his name written everywhere, in every corner, on every page meeting the intensity of Julie's love. Sometimes, he deplored, love leads to prostration.

"Rose is raving mad. She was howling from the rooftops, understand? There's something from her past in her inventions about women. I'm sure it comes from her family. It must have been something in her childhood."

Julie abruptly stopped talking, she realized how stupid what she said sounded, and realized too that she had raised her voice, attracting the attention of a number of customers, they raised their eyes and looked, then immediately returned to their laptops, most of them Macintoshes, their small white apple bitten into in the middle.

"Presented that way, I know it doesn't make for a compelling story. Every adult had a childhood in which something happened. But her story and her stylist's point of view on the world of fashion could really be interesting for the documentary. She pushes her ideas to the limit to get people worried about her condition. That's the impression she gave. It's like parents who are pedophile in their feelings, who refuse to see that the greatest gift they can give their children is to leave them room to grow."

Charles looked at Julie wearily. For the first time what she was giving off seemed suspect, malicious, a lack of heart, a hidden flaw. She was merciless in the way she attacked others. Unlike him, in her work she was a shredder, a vampire.

"Her desire for the world to be a certain way dismisses the reality of the world," she continued, softening her tone to almost a murmur, her body straining toward Charles across the table.

"If I understand correctly, you want to ridicule her in front of everyone? Make a sideshow out of her? You want us to be case studies?"

Stung by the word "us," Julie looked at Charles. With a single remark, he'd gone back to being a couple with Rose, right in front of her, and against her. It wasn't the first time she'd understood that he wasn't entirely hers, but it was the first time he showed his claws for another woman, ready to leave the embrace they'd been living in for months, and stare her down, take her on directly.

"No, that's not it, you don't understand. I don't want to ridicule her. I don't want to make you two into case studies, as you said. I want to show where you're from, your families. Have your worlds revealed, your universe. Show how your careers choices have to do with where you're from."

"Showing, revealing. Why don't you use yourself as a subject, so we can have a good laugh?"

Charles pushed her datebook away from him across the table, the way you push aside a dish you don't want anymore, to get away from its smell.

"Some things don't need your light cast on them, Julie. You can't do whatever you want with other people. Rose isn't crazy, and she isn't howling mad either. She's one of the strongest women I've met."

"Of course I can't do whatever I want with you. That's a given, you don't even need to say it. Who do you think I am? What's the matter with you? What's this business about the strongest woman?"

"I just saw Rose, just now," he told her, staring with unfocused eyes at a point in the window of Java U, where people walked past.

"She came to the studio on a whim this morning. She wants to start working with me again. She says she's ready, she's come to terms with living without me."

Charles finally turned his gaze back to Julie again, who didn't feel like talking anymore.

"It might be a good idea to take her back," he continued, taking Julie's hand in his. She took it back just as fast, hiding it under the table, a loser. Charles noted her move but decided not to make anything of it. He hated these complications between men and women, things that just weren't worth it, stupidities like interior design, some colour that didn't quite fit.

"It might be a good idea. It might not be. I want to give her a chance. Stylists like her don't come around every day."

"Women like her don't come around every day," Julie echoed, to give ominous meaning to his words.

They had nothing more to say to each other. Charles left and Julie could hear alcohol's siren's voice. She stared at her computer screen, unable to read anything on it. What she'd written meant nothing to her now. She knew she wouldn't be able to work anymore that day.

From then on, Julie felt like she was being gnawed on by rats. She began drinking again, from time to time at first, once or twice a week, then every day, only in the evenings, then in the afternoon. She hid to drink. That was useless since drinking is always visible, it's not something that can be hidden in a relationship.

Behind her apparent jealousy, another monster was lurking, far worse. Julie was worried about Charles, and that worry was something she'd never known before with men, it was related to the fetishistic pleasure he took, a pleasure she believed she could understand and share. Now she saw that her understanding of it was only ideational, answers filled with nothing more than ideas. She now knew that trying to accede to his desires could only destroy her, and though she was convinced she would destroy herself, she would continue to accept, continue to try.

For that pleasure of his, she found a word that destroyed him every time she uttered it: slaughterer.

IT WAS WINTER and it was cold. A cold as intense as the burning of summer. Cold like a row of teeth where the white smoke of the city's chimneys that followed the wind's direction seemed itself to be made of ice, about to freeze over and shatter. Montreal was at its deadest, some restaurants didn't make the effort to open, others offered passersby empty interiors where an idle waiter lazily lingered.

Julie was at Plan B with Charles and Bertrand, the latter still in a sour mood, despite the time that had passed. He couldn't accept that Julie was in a relationship with Charles, he could have tolerated it if they were just fucking, but a real story, with daily life and shared projects—that he couldn't swallow. Bertrand was in a dark mood out of allegiance to Rose, but also out of resentment, since he'd never understood why she'd chosen Charles over him, he'd never been able to cut through her coldness or generate even the slightest emotion in her. Julie only had eyes for Charles, and she removed everyone from her world with no qualms through the exclusivity she awarded him with, sickening him, it seemed too animal, unacceptable, the way she'd obliterated everything that didn't relate to Charles.

"Does Bertrand know about the slaughterer?" she asked Charles earlier that day.

"Stop it with that word! I don't want to get into it. Not with you."

"Not with me? With who then? Does Bertrand know about it, yes or no?"

"No, and he never will."

"Rose kept the secret for you all this time?"

She looked at Charles the way he'd never been looked at before, as if she were seeing him for the first time, as if she truly saw him as he was, a twisted man, to say the least.

"She never talked about it with you? Impossible. One day Bertrand will find out, and he'll judge you! And Rose will find out what you're made of too one day, and she'll judge you as well!"

But that night at Plan B she was quiet, she had no wish to exit her prostration that protected her from the others. Bertrand and

Charles were discussing something that didn't interest her, she was drinking with great application, praying for the pain to stop or at least not worsen. She was dipping her finger in her glass, drawing rings on the table when a young blond woman came up to her, attracting her attention by touching her shoulder with a hand even finer than Rose's or hers, "a paw" as they said where she came from. Julie recognized her immediately; she had never been able to forget her. She had a name for that enemy emerging from her past, from the depths of time: Girly. Steve had left her for this one, she had debased herself before her. The blond was smiling at her as if they were friends, as if she'd be searching for an opportunity to speak to her.

"I know who you are. I'm Steve Grondin's ex. Like you, I was hurt."

"Sorry? You're what?"

Julie had understood, of course, but she felt disgusted by the idea of building a bond around shared grief, sisterhood at the bottom of the barrel, that would have made Steve into an object of worship, a miserable god, true enough, but a god nonetheless.

"I'm Steve's ex. I dated him after you. It was hard for me too."

"Yeah, right. You think it's over? You think your love affairs will have better endings now?"

The blond woman retreated a step, raising her hand to push aside a strand of hair that had fallen over her eye, smoothing the end between her fingers the way injured cats lick their fur. She was hurt, and in her malaise, the way she felt ridiculed in front of witnesses, Julie saw herself as she had been, years ago, flower in hand, she pictured herself sent packing, dismissed at the Assommoir bar. Right, that's it, humiliate yourself, burn yourself on my surface, smash your face against my fist, Julie challenged

Girly in her mind, Julie was already looking elsewhere, straight ahead, drinking her drink, ignoring Girly, cancelling her out, and Girly, looking for something else to say and finding nothing, departed empty-handed from Julie's blind spot. For all the world she wouldn't have given her a sign of compassion, she left without a word and without understanding what had happened, she probably thought she was offering a flower, in her own way, to Julie. Two minutes later, Julie spotted her in the doorway, wearing a long black coat, going out the door, outside. Girly had left the building, and Julie's glass was empty.

That night, she didn't give it any more thought, but the next day the scene caught up with her, forcing a thousand thoughts into her already crowded head, a den of lions she could no longer tame, opening their maws in every direction. Again she felt imprisoned in the great wheel that dominated her, stronger than the relationship she had with Charles, a movement that echoed the disorder in the skies and the drift of continents, a movement that could accelerate, causing a colossal shift in the ocean currents. Julie came to a conclusion: to survive, it was better not to look for happiness but avoid suffering, off the wheel. You had to find cover.

VII

LIFE WITHOUT CHARLES

OUTSIDE THERE WASN'T even any snow. The temperature was far above seasonal levels, change was ineluctable, every media outlet predicted it as experts in suits and ties commented on the progressive ruin of the land that was breaking apart through every means known to nature, all at once: earthquakes, cyclones, typhoons, and a tsunami, the melting of Polar ice adrift, port cities and fertile land drowned in salt water.

In high places, predictions were falling on deaf ears, including in the White House. Soon, in the northern portion of North America, the seasons would disappear and become the same, they would soon turn into an endless magma of greyness and humidity, heat and sun out of orbit, off its trajectory and, who knows, heading on a collision course with Earth. Greenland would fall into the Atlantic Ocean, making hundreds of millions of people flee for higher ground. Autumn and winter would be characterized by mud and wind, beating rain and mental depression, spring and summer by climate-controlled shopping malls, electrical storms, weather alerts, and the agglutination of children in public pools, all pissing in the rancid water.

Like Julie O'Brien, Rose Dubois was personally affected by the weather, she'd adopted this trait of Julie's to impress Charles, in thought only because he wasn't there to see her and take pleasure in it. She couldn't please Charles anymore but she could imagine that one day she could please him, she'd do it by appropriating, one by one, all of Julie's features, in body and mind. She was wrong about what Julie was and what Charles wanted, but she couldn't know that, couldn't know what he wanted because he himself was lost, he knew nothing now, because only God, who didn't exist as One Who Intervenes, as a Professor in man's questioning, could have told him.

Outside, women were beginning to undress and show their beauty, the only beauty that remained despite the planetary imbalance, a beauty that grew through the studied and generalized practice of striptease.

Day was falling in early April, Rose was sitting in a pastry shop on Colonial Avenue, the Baguette Dorée, which was also a bakery and a café all in one, right in front of the building where she no longer lived but where she still had a few cardboard boxes, sitting safely as a pretext to return. Five or six excuses, she calculated that very day, but still she couldn't return five or six times, taking one box during each visit to bring it back to the surgeon's house. Her rigmarole was obvious but acceptable, yet as time passed it would become too obvious and unbearable for Charles, and annoying him was the last thing she wanted. To get close to him and get him back, she had to play the game of frivolity, the comedy of healing, pride proclaimed through eyes held high and an affable manner. In her case, an affable manner was a challenge because there was not much that could penetrate Ativan, an anxiolytic Dr. Gagnon prescribed her, and that spread over her life like a layer of down, a soothing medicine that nipped in the bud expressions of happiness or suffering, as Botox had before it.

Rose had a storehouse of visits that had to be carefully managed. She wanted to put off the time when there would be no more reasons to go see Charles, with or without an appointment, as an ex-girlfriend who has a right to take what is hers. She was sitting in front of a *café au lait* and a Portuguese pastry, *ovos moles* that she tore into little bits instead of eating. She'd become thinner but was still pretty, she still had her good skin that shone beneath her well-fitting clothes and the high-heel boots she was wearing were even higher than the ones she used to wear a year ago.

From the bakery she was keeping watch on the large windows of Julie's loft, on the third floor, where the drapes were pulled. With a bit of patience, Rose could catch shadows here and there, traces of Julie and Charles in profile, dancing on the ceiling. Then she let herself slip into a trance, looking for a sign that might be aimed at her, that might be for her, hurt at not being that second shadow next to Charles and grateful for the disguise these shadows represented, distancing her from them, covering up what they were doing, making the nature of their activities indefinable, or at least ambiguous. The bakery customers who liked her threw sideways glances in her direction, but they thought she was a lunatic, with the look of hysteria they couldn't understand because they did like her prettiness. That she was desperate was unthinkable to them. For men and women alike, women's beauty was incompatible with failure, hysteria, and pain. It was inconceivable that beautiful women might die young or kill themselves, simply because they were beautiful; it was intolerable that they might destroy themselves, that beauty might be damaged by the beautiful woman herself, that this beauty might not be a natural resource, a public good protected by the laws of men. In this widely shared perspective, only ordinary or ugly women could fail, kill themselves or be murdered, they had a right to despair because their degradation was comprehensible, a consequence of the banality of their appearance, or their ugliness, which came down to the same thing: anything that departed from beauty, in women, even a little, fell into a no man's land.

Rose was absent-mindedly watching the windows of Julie's loft which were now dark, though the drapes had been drawn from the inside unbeknownst to her, indicating that someone had been there a while, lying low in obscurity. But nothing was happening, she had to be patient, maybe another *café au lait*, tearing another pastry apart with her fingers.

Outside, dirt and wet. What was left of the snow couldn't be called snow since its nature had long separated from that white fluffy material, volatile and cottony that covered her country for centuries, giving it its reputation, the source of its folklore; now, through metamorphosis snow had become a black crust mixed in with mud. Montreal the Sow was dirtier than ever and her cleaners, the blue-collar workers, were once again on strike. They were using grime as a pressure tactic against Montrealers who would have to accede to their demands for higher wages. Society's well-being was held hostage by garbage men who stuck the citizens' clean noses in their own shit, and the city looked like a garbage dump even worse than New York, Rose thought that day, though she'd never been to New York.

As she was numbly considering the bottom of her coffee cup, a light flashed on at Julie O'Brien's place. Rose was electrified, for her it was like a curtain rising, an entanglement revealed, the beginning of a play. A shadow appeared, then moved over the ceiling and paced a moment, disappeared, reappeared and disappeared again, at regular intervals. A second shadow approached the first, this one calmer, indolent, as if bored with the other's fever, its nervous fidgeting. Rose felt a disagreement between the two shadows, and pleasure burned inside her, she was witnessing the couple's first argument projected on the ceiling like two shadow puppets, a tearful woman and a man accused. Then the light went out the way it first came on, without warning.

Barely a minute later, the couple appeared in the street, Julie in front and Charles behind. Julie was crying and walking quickly, like a woman who wants to flee as she waits to be held back, forcing her man to play a part, the guy who doesn't want her to go. She was walking toward the café where Rose sat, a danger for Rose, she had to jump up and turn around and hide from Julie, while trying to keep an eye on her as she walked by. Julie stopped in front of Baguette Dorée's storefront, where Charles caught up with her. The bakery employees looked on incredulously as Rose hid behind a shelf stacked with fresh bread, but the show was worth the price of admission. Yes, that was Julie's shadow that had paced the ceiling, growing ever more irritated with Charles' stoic nature, Rose recognized her Charles, still breathtakingly beautiful, even if he needed a haircut.

Rose had seen the couple once walking in the street, side by side, and she'd seen Charles and Julie walking separately, though neither had seen her, she instinctively knew how to act with self-effacement, she slipped to the other side of the street, slowed her pace, sat down on a bench, took a detour, using a shop for cover. Seeing them individually or together devastated her every time, but on this afternoon, a fault line opened up in the way the couple presented itself to the world: Charles had remained unchanged while Julie seemed damaged, smaller in every part of her body, a Russian doll emerging from her big sister, set next to her, a diminutive double, on the mantelpiece.

Julie had lost weight, but more than her body was involved, her face spoke, she wore no makeup, deep circles sagged under her eyes and her white skin was blemished, reddened in spots.

Charles was trying to get her to hold still by grabbing her arm, but Julie was fighting him, at first energetically, then more slowly, finally she yielded by putting her arms around his neck, though her left arm seemed unable to straighten out completely. Rose could see something Julie couldn't: Charles' bored look, a look eloquent with disappointment, which Rose knew all too well. Then the couple separated after they kissed, blandly, with no heat. Charles went toward Saint Lawrence Boulevard, hands in his pockets, a spiteful expression on his face, while Julie moved off toward their building with the slowness of souls in purgatory.

Rose left her shelter behind the bread rack and sat back down at the table that gave onto Colonial Avenue. A smile on her lips, she began anew to tear up her *ovos moles* and drink small sips of her second *café au lait*, still piping hot. Then, turning to face the street, she found herself looking directly at Julie who was standing stock-still and straight in front of the window, staring at her, her face hard and wet tears still on her cheeks, her expression in pain but still haughty so that nothing could impress, terrible because it was indestructible underneath the veneer of humiliation. The shock of seeing Julie in the window was so great that Rose dropped her cup with a noise that again attracted the attention of the staff: the two women facing each other, staring like children raised by wolves at their reflection in a mirror. Julie had caught Rose red-handed. She knew Rose wasn't there by chance, she'd been coming there for a while, she'd become a regular there, it was a scheme to spy on her and Charles. She turned on her heels and walked toward her loft like a mechanical approximation of a woman, while Rose, who had failed to hide through sheer idiotic satisfaction, began getting her things together to leave, still in shock, unsteady on her high-heeled boots. She would never be able to return to the bakery but that didn't matter. As the light slowly ebbed over the starry mantle of the sky, she'd gotten her money's worth, and it would keep her for a while.

THE RESTAURANT CALLED Chez L'Épicier in Old Montreal was Marc Gagnon's favourite, with its choices of surprising dishes like a strawberry dessert topped with calamari mousse. According to Marc, nothing could exceed the delight of eating there accompanied by a beautiful young woman like Rose, who'd suddenly come into his life, in the middle of the night, just at the right time, though he'd been thinking of her for a while.

He had just separated from his wife with whom he had no children, and had stopped touching long ago.

At a table at the back of the restaurant, near the majestic staircase covered in red carpet that led to the toilets, five women were speaking very loudly, celebrating someone's birthday. They were all between forty and fifty, they were talking, eating, drinking, laughing, winking, and glancing around, but no dice.

But Rose wasn't thinking about the life around her. She was still considering the scene she'd witnessed two weeks earlier, which had finally convinced her to quit Ativan, slowly, under Marc's supervision, since he was well aware that her dependence on the anxiolytic was keeping her close to him, it made her dependent on his prescription pad. He was a bridge, he knew, between Rose and what she wanted, and what Rose wanted was to fight for Charles with Marc's help, take advantage of Julie's weakness to do battle with her and send her sprawling to the mat.

The night she had called him and gone to his place, Marc welcomed her kindly, she didn't even need to explain why. He was happy to learn that her man had left her for another woman, and that he didn't love Rose anymore. Marc's ability to leave her in her silences that could last hours at a time, without forcing himself into them, without worrying, was a true gift to Rose, who more than anything needed to be alone with someone.

"Do you know what's happening in Vietnam right now?" she asked him over dinner, cutting a vegetable in her plate, some sort of strange red carrot she'd never seen and whose name was unknown, a cross between two roots.

"A revolution? A coup?"

"No. Well, maybe. That's not what I mean."

Rose reached for the bottle of wine, a Cahors, but Marc anticipated her desire and pre-empted her with a clean move, a surgeon's hand, in all circumstances.

"It's due to economic growth, the newspapers say," she continued, watching her glass being filled.

"Overnight, women have turned to plastic surgery in droves. It's become massive in such a short time. Men set themselves up as surgeons, and beauty salons open unauthorized clinics in their backrooms. Drop-in clinics, of course. Women are disfigured, or wake up with two different eyelids. But no matter, they go ahead, without thinking. They want to be operated on as quickly as possible. They turn down anaesthetics to save time. To go faster, to get back to work."

Marc Gagnon didn't like talking about work outside of his office, even indirectly, especially if he was eating, and more so if he was eating something he had difficulty identifying with certainty. He would have to get Rose to understand this at some point, but each thing in its own time, nothing needed to be hurried, the night was still young.

"Asians in general lack self-criticism," he answered after a time. "Always top speed, eyes closed. People like that scare me. They'll submit to Order, no matter if Order keeps changing its face. They're all about accomplishment, movement without reflection. I've heard that humanities, like psychology or philosophy, don't exist over there."

"These women are operated on at top speed," she continued, not taking the trouble to listen to him. "Some of them catch infections because there's no sterilization of instruments. Getting operated on or putting on lipstick, it's all the same. Getting sewn up is the same as getting made-up."

Sewing, she'd said. Sewing is like patching. Marc Gagnon hated when she used that word around him, since he'd done everything she'd wanted for years, he had been many things but certainly not a seamstress, or a tailor, his talent had nothing to do with stitches and the patching of wounds. Another thing he would have to tell her, very soon, in time.

"I'm starting to believe the Western world is sick," she continued. "I think the East is clearly demonstrating that."

"It's true that Western women are getting operated on at a

faster clip. Though it certainly isn't as fast or as all-encompassing as Asians."

"I'm sure that every day in the West, women are disfigured. By their own eagerness. Through their exaggeration."

"No doubt. Surgeons have to be vigilant, they have a code of ethics. Some of the women who come in for plastic surgery have pretty wild ideas."

"You've probably operated on them, right?"

"It's happened, sure. Two weeks ago, there was a case. I operated on a young woman who, in my opinion, was a prostitute or worked in porno. Her demands are always pretty extravagant."

Marc stopped talking, and fell to stabbing at small pieces of fennel with his fork.

"Really? What sort of demands?" Rose insisted.

"We're eating. Talking about it might spoil your appetite."

"I'm asking."

"Well, I started by performing vaginoplasty to tighten her vaginal walls."

The women at the far table burst out laughing, and Marc stopped and looked around to make sure no one was listening. Then he continued his explanations.

"It's a laser operation that makes the inside of the vagina more narrow through cauterization. The procedure is becoming more widespread. But that's not all. She wanted me to operate on her inner labia so that they would be absorbed by the outer. Like the vagina of a little girl."

The waiter who had come up and heard "the vagina of a little girl" issue from Marc Gagnon's mouth froze, with one arm extended toward the wine bottle he hadn't touched. Not knowing whether to serve them or question them, he decided to take out a small brush and clean the table, pushing crumbs into one hand, then hurrying away.

"You can see why I don't like talking about surgery in public."

"Who cares? Please, tell me more."

"Before the operation, she got her pubic hair removed by laser. The depilation is definitive and provides maximum visibility of her genitals. Personally, I think that's going too far," he continued. "At the same time, there is no risk of disfigurement. It's not her face. The face is public, and genitals are private."

Then time stopped, and the restaurant disappeared. Just then, at Chez L'Épicier in Old Montreal, Rose was certain that her story, the one she was sharing with Julie and Charles no matter how physically distant they were from her, had been predetermined, governed by a force superior to hers, superior to Marc as well, whom she didn't really consider except insofar as his past had made him a plastic surgeon. As she listened to Marc's story of the woman with the labia cut and then tightened, the inner lips swallowed by the outer, drawn tight and concealed from prying eyes, Rose was struck by a revelation, a solution for the life she'd always led, the possibility of acquiring the right pussy, of the right shape, a priceless treasure, key to all men's desire. Just then she knew she would be able, through Marc, to get a key, *the* key, the ultimate lure that would force Charles back to her, the lure she had been missing and that he might be dreaming of, in secret, filled with shame.

Rose felt she was floating above herself. A great wind had risen in her mind, blowing every which way and, outside of that, her ideas buffeted about were slowly organizing themselves like migratory birds, ideas that had become a direction, and nothing else mattered. As astounding as the lightning strike on the roof last summer, this operation would be her way of getting Charles back, even if it was only to extract his sperm, even it was only for that, to receive his cock, to get fucked.

Rose was staring at Marc, unseeing; she saw something else. Her own pussy, made to measure.

"No," Marc said emphatically.

He had stopped eating, and placed his knife and fork next to his plate.

"The answer is no."

"No, what?"

"No, I won't agree to operate on you. Not there."

Marc had guessed her intentions, anticipated her desire, as he'd done earlier in the evening with the wine. Rose had no desire to play the naïve role, and besides, she was far away, far from the restaurant and Marc, imagining her new pussy, tight and girlish, with no hair, a pussy evolving through the healing process, a perfect one, a lovely bite, a mouthful.

"Well, someone else will, then," she decided, staring straight at him, seeing him weaken for the first time.

They finished their meal in silence. To reassure Marc, who felt he was losing his grip on her, and make him forget her cold determination that showed how she was using him, Rose took his hand in hers and held it a long time, saying the words that were needed for forgiveness.

In the weeks that followed, Rose did not mention the operation. She knew Marc would operate on her when the time came; he would because he loved her, she knew that he would go against his own will for her, he would pursue the madness that wasn't yet his, but would soon be.

Rose was walking down Saint Lawrence Boulevard, earphones on her ears, another habit she'd gotten from Julie, not even listening to the music eating away at her eardrums, and that the sea of passersby could hear in a five-metre radius, they turned in her direction to identify the source of the noise, squealing metal produced by an endless electric guitar solo from an old ZZ Top hit, "Sharp Dressed Man."

A few weeks earlier she went by Charles' studio, and surprised him with a visit. He was at his computer, retouching photos, and he had welcomed her with a smile and even a little nervousness, like a sign of regret, a slight shiver, since here was a person who had disappeared and suddenly returned, and been missed in the interim. She offered to start working for him again as a stylist. She was over him, she lied, she accepted he was with Julie as long as Julie would stay away from the studio, at least for now. She hadn't worked in months but had taken time off to think, and understand things, to learn about life. Their team shouldn't end with their love affair, that would be a waste.

She hid nothing from him. She was still living with a man and would stay with him until she got back on her feet, he had to understand that much. Hadn't he thrown her out in the middle of the night and humiliated her? Had he thought so little of her when he deprived her of her relationship, her loft, and her job? What had she done to deserve such betrayal? Charles told her he regretted that it had ended the way it did, through an ugly act that she didn't deserve. He didn't understand how it happened either, looking back. He couldn't remember what had come over him, and he'd been thinking about it a lot.

At one point Charles left the studio to grab his lunch that the Meat Market, a popular local restaurant, made for him. Rose used the opportunity to go through Charles' computer, since she knew it by heart. Very quickly, she found what she was looking for: the porn sites he had visited the day before, each one proof that Julie wasn't the Woman, she didn't have it All, she didn't own the ultimate Pussy. The images were still the same, mysterious in their selection, fear-inducing for those who weren't like Charles, or in love with Charles. Charles hadn't changed. In the parade of women through his life he remained unaltered, his body aged like everyone else, but his being was frozen in time, he remained a small child.

A child's sex for a child. That's what she wanted for herself, that's what she was about to acquire, then offer him. The operation was to take place in early May in a clinic where Marc didn't usually operate. His team knew he was with Rose, and the idea certainly didn't appeal to his staff. Having a relationship with a female patient stunk of perversion as it was, and if word about his next procedure with her was to spread, the Canadian Society of Plastic Surgeons might be alerted, and he might be reprimanded and considered a moral degenerate.

She walked swiftly toward Salon Furisme, her new hairdresser, and the place where a number of Montreal's stars got their hair done and where she was forever changing her look with Marc's money, too often, it was another one of her compulsions, cutting her hair shorter and shorter. As she walked, she thought about how she might get Charles to see her Pussy and get Julie into the picture as well, making her see the desire in his eyes and the electricity that would burn there, but also the instant when Charles would spring from deep inside himself and let the beast loose, the way he'd done in front of her, Rose, at Julie's loft that fateful night. Rose wondered whether she should physically push Julie to the scene of the unveiling of the Pussy, the way statues of famous men are presented at a ceremony, or whether it was enough for Julie to just see a picture of it, or better, a video.

As she walked down Saint Lawrence Boulevard, an image sprung unbidden from her memory. She saw herself as a child in a wooden shed with two little neighbours, boys, their pants around their ankles, and she looking at the boys' organs as they looked at hers. The image was clear, distinct, banal. Very quickly another image followed: she and her four sisters in the bathtub, packed in like sardines, her little brother, it seemed, was in her arms—he was no more than a babe-in-arms who might drown. Rose thought of the image of six children naked in the bathtub, the family taking their bath, the group dominated by the sex of the babe-in-arms with the little girls holding him like a trophy, as if they had given birth to him themselves. Another image followed, this one long forgotten and producing its anxiety, an image of suffering: her mother Rosine crying, naked as well, in the bathroom but not in the tub, sitting on the toilet seat, a hazy image of Rosine naked and crying, sitting on the toilet, stronger still, the unfocused vision of her body in tatters, her breasts damaged by feeding, her mother crying, moaning, repeating Rose's cursed name, Rosine repeating Rose, Rose, my little Rose, and Rose not knowing what to do with this overflowing of tears and flesh, she didn't know why her mother was crying so hard and so loud. Rose took the pain upon herself with its mysterious cause, the sadness she might have been responsible for, she couldn't remember clearly. Another image travelled through time to her: she was a little girl being pulled down the aisle of an airplane away from the bathroom, her underwear was around her ankles and her mother Rosine was pulling her, "Mom, Mom, stop," but Rosine paid no attention, maybe because she knew nothing about underwear around her knees, maybe because she considered that demanding to have your underwear on was a childish whimsy when you were like Rose, a hairless child in a plane, in the middle of the sky, too young for modesty.

Rose put up no resistance to the images rushing through her; she let the flow continue. Hundreds of images passed through her, interlocking, falling one into the other, some instantaneous, like pictures of her as a teenager spending hours in front of the mirror, hours and hours spent scrutinizing every inch of her face and body, trying on different clothes and applying makeup, weighing herself, doing her hair and waxing herself, dressing and making up her sisters who, as they got older, moved away one after the other, leaving the clan of females and cleaving to males, going toward them like escape routes. The everyday images of her mother sitting in the living room in front of the tv after Renald Dubois, her father, left, memories of her past friendships followed, friends and roommates in various apartments and at various parties, in bars and restaurants, images of Kathleen, a childhood friend who showed her breasts in public and had the entire high school at her feet, next came the photo shoots, hundreds of models' bodies one on top of the other, like a painting of the fall from grace into the depths of hell, a collection of shoots and magazines, pornographic images as well that Charles collected on the Internet, pictures of Charles in bed with her, Charles and Julie in bed, witnessed and imagined, images from tv, her and Marc Gagnon in bed, his strange body that wasn't like Charles', ending in the vaginoplasty she'd seen the day before, in a Polaroid that Marc kept in a folder.

Rose had walked past Furisme without realizing it, she was going too fast, blinded, as if the surface of the world around her that offered so much had lost its physical shape, its colour.

All images had a common theme. Sex. Sex was central to her life and life in general, it was the thread that held all lives together. It was wrong to say that you were born from a pussy because you never left it. It was wrong to say that everything in life comes back to sex because it was never far enough from sex to return to it, life never went anywhere else, life was a prisoner of sex from beginning to end, even the lives of children. Sex was the only place life lived, from the cradle on.

The revelation depressed her so much she stopped walking and sat down on a bench. She wouldn't go to the salon to get her hair cut. She wouldn't get a new colour either, and she wouldn't go to the gym. She wished she could have decided not to sacrifice herself on the operating table, but that was impossible. Her decision was irrevocable and it wasn't even hers, a force bigger than her had decided, and it had swallowed her up.

VIII

NATURE'S REVENGE

JULIE O'BRIEN WAS running on the treadmill at the over-crowded Nautilus. Members had to keep an eye on the equipment like vultures, they crowded around the machines and determined who would go next, in civilized fashion they organized the pecking order of benches, bars, and weights. Everyone had to alternate, it was the law of the land in times of over-crowding which came, every year, with spring, when the entire city was trying to get back into shape, the season of short shorts and hormones, when you showed off your body.

Her head ached but Julie ran anyway, trying unsuccessfully to imagine herself on stage with fans all around her, calling out her name, her Star's name. In her relationship with Charles, she'd lost even this pitiful means of auto-congratulation that so often softened the blow of existence.

Her shoulder wasn't in a sling anymore but she still couldn't work her muscles with free weights, that caused too much pain, but no matter, time was short and she was running, earphones on, listening to Madonna's "Jump," trying to find that state of grace again, that calm assurance she had before Charles came and tore down everything in her life. She was running to recapture what she'd lost.

There were mirrors everywhere in the white neon lighting,

an abrasive, pitiless light. She was emaciated with dark circles under her eyes, her gauntness gave her a tragic air. You couldn't really say that her gauntness made her uglier, but it took away her sexual aura, her lioness attitude. Now you could see her without noticing her, and she didn't notice anyone either, she'd lost sight of herself, her face was secluded from the world. Her hair had grown out and her roots showed strawberry blond, visible in what was left of her platinum colour, so much that they looked brown. In the street, men had stopped turning around to look at her, or less than before, she was melting into Montreal and its crowds who had to step around the lampposts that lit up gutted streets, potholes more like craters that revealed the sewers, open maws that contributed to the ruin of the city.

She'd gotten into the habit of drinking every day from afternoon onward, always vodka or white wine, when it wasn't both. But she wasn't going to continue, she had prepared a plan to limit the damage. First, she would get her appetite back through physical exercise and giving up alcohol; once her appetite returned, her sleep patterns would normalize, and once she slept better she would simply follow the program she'd prepared to recover the pride she'd had as a dominant woman, an Alpha Female. She would act upon her life, she wouldn't let herself die a second time, she'd promised herself that much, it was better to kill herself once and for all, or kill someone else.

Her affair with Charles was a misunderstanding. She should have seen it from the start, she knew it was impossible for anyone, man or woman, to recover from great trauma in the past, she knew that a child's redemption from insane parents was only a story you told yourself, another lie gladly spoken. She should have known, she knew from the start that Charles was a fashion photographer, and she had encountered early on the deviancy through which he found pleasure, and she had gone so far as to love it.

After an hour on the treadmill, Julie decided to leave the overcrowded gym for Java U, to eat and write.

From Charles and photography, she moved on to another subject associated with it, closer to women in general and herself in particular, a subject that would certainly raise interest among Quebec's larger television networks. She'd gotten a producer to read a description of the project, and following a discussion, he decided to send the document out. Not long after, they were called to pitch the idea to Radio-Canada, everyone at the table knew them, she had a reputation, one that wasn't all good. She wanted to talk about images as cages, in a world where women, more and more naked, more and more photographed, covered themselves in lies, they had to find ever more fantastic means, spend greater sums of time and money and pain, use technical and medical means to build masks, substitute their bodies with an infallible uniform, impermeable, with the passage of time they risked going too far and becoming monsters like Michael Jackson, Cher, and Donatella Versace. In all societies, from the most traditional to the most liberal, women's bodies couldn't be shown, or not really, not the real body. The real body of women remained unbearable, fundamentally disturbing. When this unbearable side turned to obsession, each and every woman took the most extreme means to treat the illness, means to destruction or infinite manipulation, always to control men's erections, the absolute core of human society.

In that context, Charles couldn't hold centre stage, he became just a creator of images, a manufacturer of uniforms. Besides, love and its related states didn't interest her in writing, her motor was indignation, an emotion far more stable and durable, where the forces of proclamation intervened.

Julie was fleshing out these ideas when a hand fell upon on her shoulder, a small, soft, moist hand that touched her without touching her, with disdain. Julie looked up, already weary and annoyed.

"Hello, Julie. You're pale. You look out of shape."

Rose was standing there. She was tanned and elegantly dressed, without that haggard air the time she'd been caught at the Baguette Dorée. Rose had that fresh self-confidence women have when they stand before others uglier than they are, others whose mental distress can be read in the pallor of their skin.

"How strange. You showed up just as I was writing about you. Since you've been away, you've become my protagonist."

Rose was stunned. Of all potential replies, she hadn't prepared for that one.

"Oh, really? So Charles left?"

"I pushed him out. Out of my script, not my life. Sit down, let's talk."

"I was just going by when I saw you. I've got other things to do."

"I don't believe you. Something tells me you're here for a reason. I don't know why."

An employee opened the door to get some fresh air into the café and kept it open with a hook, letting the noise of the street pour in.

"Ever since the Baguette Dorée, I get the feeling you're hanging around," Julie continued.

Outside, tires screeched, then came the noise of a collision between two cars. Everyone in the café turned, except Julie and Rose. Customers moved toward the window and exchanged their opinions, all except Rose and Julie, trapped in their duel.

"First, it isn't true. Second, if you want to tell me something, I don't need to be sitting down."

"As you like. The subject of fashion photography has moved toward the torturing of the body as something that needs to be illuminated. I'm thinking of the title *The Burqa of Skin* for a documentary. It could tell the story of women who bury their bodies through relentless aesthetic efforts."

Outside, people had gathered on the sidewalks, watching the increasingly hectic traffic caused by the accident. Rose stood with her mouth open, unable to adjust to the situation.

"I'll never be part of that. You're crazy."

"Wait. Let me finish. I could be in it too."

"Then it'll be worse."

"I thought we could be Charles' models. We could do a shoot together that would be filmed by a cameraman I know. For the documentary, the actual shoot would be the subject, more than the pictures themselves."

Life was tightening around Rose, the movements of the sky continued to indicate the path to follow, events were making a way for her, she just needed to let herself go. That's what destiny was, to be carried along by the current, helping it gain speed, letting yourself float in all your glory, like Ophelia. The idea of a shoot and her as a model, even if she wasn't alone, added to the prospect of her modified pussy. A light lit up in Rose's eyes, one that Julie had predicted—and noticed.

"We could wait for the sun, the month of July, and meet on the roof again. Think about it."

"Whatever. But I doubt it," Rose answered out of principle.

Then Rose smiled, thinking of how Julie would react when she gazed upon her Pussy. More than ever, she hated her.

CHARLES WAS IN his studio, in front of the computer whose screen displayed parts of women's bodies on which he clicked to zoom in on and observe every detail. He had a stubborn erection but he couldn't get himself to come. In his whole life, he'd never felt so weary, of himself and the world that had given birth to him. Rose wasn't there to help carry the burden of shame and disgust, she wasn't there and she'd been replaced by Julie, who had him by the balls.

He resented her for constantly making him feel ashamed of his tastes, he resented her for the way she made him feel that his pleasures were a pathology, always bringing back this business with his father, bringing the old man into their bed, where he was least welcome. Unlike Julie, Rose wasn't a bomb about to go off, nor was she constantly judging. And she didn't have that past as an alcoholic and didn't let herself drift off the same way, pain didn't have the same power of destruction over her, pain causing death.

Of the two women, Rose was best for him, even if she was less passionate than Julie. But when he thought about it, he really just wanted to be alone, he wanted neither Rose nor Julie, it was time to move on to something completely different, a string of one-night stands while he was still young, barely thirty years old.

At least that's what he thought he wanted, but he wasn't sure about anything when it came to his future and women. Charles wasn't feeling right, and he didn't understand why. It wasn't because Rose was gone, and it wasn't Julie, not really. It wasn't Julie but it was something to do with her, her state, what she said to him, the way he felt her spiralling down to a place he had escaped from, but just barely, when he was younger. He hadn't been feeling right ever since Julie had started going wrong, there was no doubt, she had a kind of sorcery that made him anxious, black magic that punished his desires with pain and insults, shouts and sermons.

Charles was still looking at the screen, his hand on his cock, but he wasn't seeing the images anymore. A great malaise had come over him the day Julie made her first scene, shouting in his loft in the middle of the afternoon, already drunk and in tears, ranting about what he was doing in his studio with his fashion models and his computer, what he was doing behind her back, she waited all day for him and depended on him so much. She was pacing around the apartment, throwing pillows every which way, pieces of crumpled paper, books she'd gotten her hands on, terrorizing her three cats who'd hid under the bed, three Siamese bundles with blue eyes that watched their step, sensing the storm. She went on and on about her own father, a true Irishman who never cheated on her mother, her father, she yelled, looking at the ceiling as if she were speaking to God himself, was the man who'd loved her most in the world, who had loved her so much that everyone else was just a disappointment, ready to sacrifice her, she continued to rage.

She was sure he needed help, he needed to *see someone*, a horrible expression Charles despised, *see* like looking through, like an exam, a subject of a study. Then she said she would die, and nothing less, then swore to him, her finger pointing at him in anger, that she would never, ever let herself be controlled, this time she would stand her ground. She threatened him with one idea after another, tumbling out, talking about his computer she hoped to destroy, blow up, throw out the window.

Charles had only one thought: run away. Get out of sight of this insanity unfolding before him like a production, a play. It strangled him, it was a scene of suffocation, insanity far less insane than his own father but it was strangely similar, it grew in intensity with the same immoderation, spreading itself everywhere, the opposite of breathing, the opposite of love and desire. All that was missing were mutant creatures and G-men, the destruction of humanity glimpsed in tea leaves and the Earth as well; all that was missing was an eye in the pussy designed to watch him and keep him under surveillance.

Since that day, he started having problems sleeping and even eating. He wasn't finishing his meals, he ate only fish and vegetables and barely any at that—mastication required such concentration. At night he'd wake up with his father Pierre in mind, and Diane and Marie-Claude too. He had a bad feeling about his mother and his sister—perhaps they were in danger. Instead of worrying about Julie, he worried about his family, as if Julie, in her anguish, threatened his family. Julie demanded his attention, but she was only the door that opened onto his memories and adolescent terror. She was his nightmare.

"You're sick!" she would scream at him, and those words made him feel cold all over, a nameless fear, noises and doubts, intentions hidden behind the physical world, cancerous, manipulative, knowing.

There was no logic behind these new feelings that quickly turned into unshakable convictions, then premonitions. He called his mother a number of times to try and see how she was doing, and each time she attempted to calm him, each time he felt she was hiding something from him because of a word, the tone of her voice, because of noises in the background where something, he was sure, was hidden, ready to harm, he couldn't say what, but he felt something was ready to harm, like an oracle hidden in the closet. Whatever she told him, he heard something else.

He was surprised to learn that Marie-Claude went to live in the United States, in Connecticut, for six months, to learn English, the same story his father had invented to keep him away from his mother and sister, a story in which he, Charles, would leave for a year to learn English in Connecticut, in the United States, which was a complete lie. When he told his mother that the stories coincided, and that the resemblance was hard to believe, she admitted as much, she told him it was strange, she herself had thought about it and it had troubled her, but what could she do, after all Connecticut was the state that welcomed the greatest number of Quebeckers in English immersion. His sister was going there, it had all been organized, she would be there next month, she'd found a family with an American girl her age, that girl would come to Quebec later on for French immersion.

Then he learned, once again from Diane, that Pierre, who'd been at the Robert-Giffard Psychiatric Hospital for the past fifteen years, would soon be released, like many other patients. Nobody knew exactly when, but it would be soon. He could be released any day now to go and live in a pre-selected apartment not far from the hospital, held there in case he relapsed, a sure thing for severe cases like his, since he lived under tight surveillance, surrounded by powerful enemies.

Charles couldn't believe that his father, whom he hadn't seen in eight years and who, on his end, didn't seem to recognize anyone anymore, could live in the real world with his delirium and imprecations and, who knows, even track down ghosts, which might include his mother, his sister, and himself.

In the studio, the temperature was dropping; outside the wind beat against the large windows hidden by drapes. On his computer screen were still pieces of women fallen into obsolescence, worn threadbare by past masturbation. Charles knew what he had to do: go hunting, find new parts.

An hour and a half later, he ejaculated three miserable drops on his screen. He released his seed in small dry pleasure, woeful, with great sadness in his heart, weary, so lacking in pleasure that for a moment he thought of beating Julie to the punch and throwing his computer on the ground.

CHARLES WAS HOLDING Julie's hand. She had cried a long time on her brown leather couch where he liked to take her, when he wasn't doing it on the floor, on the hardwood. Besides firm bodies, he liked feeling cramped in bed, he hated having sex in the softness of mattresses and the flickering light of candles, he liked the constraint of a hard surface.

"You're sick," she was saying, "but I don't know what to do with your sickness. I just know it's impossible to cure, it's too deep. Your sickness is a god that orders you around. I'm not made to obey it. I want to give myself to a man, not a sickness, even if it comes from you. Even if it's your god."

Charles couldn't stand the words anymore, Julie felt as much. She was tired of hearing herself think them. It was hard for her to describe the situation in words, usually she talked too much and made people think she knew everything. She felt terrible, but wouldn't give up and admit defeat. What she wanted, even more than to be loved, was to fight and resist, show she was stronger than him by breaking down his limits, no matter what.

"Being in a relationship with you means engaging in self-harm. It means intentionally hurting myself."

"I'm not asking anything of you. You talk like I was forcing you to stay here."

They were sitting side by side, looking at the lemon still in the lemon tree, not yet fallen, yellow, enormous, bigger than a tennis ball.

"But I want to be able to give you something."

"I know, I'm sorry. But stop pushing. And please stop drinking because of it, I beg of you."

After these sorts of discussions—more and more frequent—Julie calmed down most of the time and would set out to seduce him, squeeze an erection out of him with the same tools that made them ashamed and that she endlessly brought back to the table, after they "consumed," after she'd been to the "slaughterer's," she told him cynically.

Julie didn't consent the way Rose had, but in a way she went further. She didn't try to cause him to swell through plastic surgery alone—no, she was an innovator, she knew she had to push her body toward ugliness, and not beauty, splendour, and health.

In the past weeks, she'd cut herself of her own volition, first her breasts, then between her legs, with a razor blade, opening dozens of deep cuts in her skin and daring Charles to take his pleasure there.

Her wounds threw Charles into ecstasy, then he paid for it with deep, disturbing distress. Shame, always shame like a mirror discovering a slab of meat, magnifying it, rigor mortis that didn't stop him and that Julie overcame, as a challenge, to hurt him too, he who gave into her initiative and her trap. Fucking her was like throwing himself into the devil's jaws.

That night, after the argument, Julie decided to return to submissiveness, as a strategy, a ruse, then something that had never happened before occurred. Julie lay flat on her back on the floor, open, her breasts overflowing from the bra she was wearing that was far too tight. Fresh cuts showed angry red on her breasts from being pinched and scratched and maintained. On her left shoulder she still had the fading yellow bruises of her former injury that gave her skin a sickly tone. Everywhere else her skin was white, almost translucent, brindled with brown tones, and her emaciated body and vacant eyes made him feverish.

His erection was solid, and it reassured him. He touched the cuts with his fingers, and scratched at them to test the firmness of the implant on the other breast, then concentrated on her wounds again. A few minutes passed and then, without warning, as he played out the performance he knew by heart and had executed a thousand times, a scene he'd always been a part of, developed to perfection, integrated into his world, his logic, his mechanical preferences, Julie slid away from him—he could see the wounds on her breasts, he could see her breasts, face, her body, but from kilometres away. Her body cast him out, distanced him, though Julie had done nothing at all, she had remained in the requisite motionless state, eyes closed, passive, a corpse.

For the first time, Charles was seeing Julie's naked body and it was a crude expression of nudity, fear-inducing, sickening like Truth. For the first time he encountered its brutality, the cold matter of it, without a purpose, without intention, nothing, an object, a flat tire. That thing did not beckon him to her, it felt neither pleasure nor displeasure, but Charles felt something he had never encountered before until after the act: disgust. Suddenly he lost his erection and even wiped the fingers that had touched the cut on his shorts, then he got up from the couch and looked around, lost.

"Charles? What's happening?"

Julie emerged from her corpse role and guessed from Charles' stunned look what was happening. She was both disappointed and relieved.

"You've been freed. You can become normal, or you can go crazy."

Charles sat back on the brown couch, holding his head in his hands. His cock lolled like a dog's tongue on a summer day, peeking out of his jeans. But there was nothing comical about it, it was sadness itself that hung there, an example, a man hanged in a town square. He felt like crying, but couldn't. He'd been beaten, destroyed. He didn't know if a treasure had been taken from him, or a splinter removed from his foot, he knew only that, for him, there would be a before and an after, no matter what that meant. In his familiar ritual, he had seen Julie, but also felt seen himself, for the first time. Now he was cold, sitting on the couch, he looked at himself the way you sometimes watch your life, in a countdown, realizing you fucked up, that you were wrong about everything the whole time.

Julie put on a bathrobe. She went to Charles and took him in her arms, her left shoulder still aching.

"Sorry," he murmured.

"I'm sorry too," she replied. "We'll have to talk about what we're going to do with our relationship. We can't continue hurting each other."

"You're right. But I'm not sure I'm happy to have known you. You need to know that. I'm sorry if I hurt you, but I resent you. Your problem. It was your problem. You've set up a judge inside me."

"You already had that judge. Everyone has one, you have to let it judge you. It's better that way."

Charles moved away from Julie, he looked at her, her new ugliness did not attract him. Julie gazed at him in return and saw a confused little boy, adorable in his remorse. She still held one of his knees in her hand despite their distance. They didn't love each other anymore, maybe they'd never loved each other. At best they'd crossed paths and spent some good times together, but that time was up, it had scraped the bottom of the barrel with Charles becoming impotent.

"There's something I want to do."

"You want to sleep at your place tonight?"

"Yes, that would be best. We'll talk tomorrow. But that's not what I wanted to say."

Charles stood and zipped himself up. He walked to the lemon tree, then slapped the lemon hard, almost knocking the tree over in its terracotta pot, sending out a shower of dirt. He barely managed to right the tree. To their surprise, the lemon didn't fall, it bounced on the end of its stem among the shaken leaves.

"What the hell is up with this lemon?" he asked with a smile.

"An unwilling fruit," she replied, grateful for the comic relief.

Charles pulled on the lemon, but couldn't tear it from its branch.

"I don't believe it, how hard can it be to pick a lemon?"

"It's a little diabolical, I think."

With the unyielding lemon taunting him, Charles got a pair of scissors from the kitchen and cut it out of the tree. He held it in one hand at eye level, triumphant, examining it closely like a curious animal.

"It's edible?"

"Absolutely. You can keep it, as a souvenir of us," Julie said. All she wanted was for this to be done, and to be alone again.

Charles left with the lemon in his coat pocket, still looking lost. Julie didn't know when she would see him again and didn't feel bad about that, quite the opposite, maybe she was stronger than she looked. She spent the next hours cleaning house. Then she ran herself a bath and watched television from under the bubbles in the tub.

Tomorrow she'd get her hair done, she'd get back on the treadmill, go back to the weights, her stage, and she'd become a Star again.

IX

CONVICTION

Rose Dubois was lying on her back. She was counting from one to ten.

Around her there was movement, peoplé she couldn't see, noises, voices heard through the rolling of a stretcher not far away, maybe in the corridor, the slamming of a door she couldn't see either. As she counted, she watched the ceiling dilute, open onto a void, a ceiling of numb cotton that lowered upon her like a shroud. The ceiling was lowering and she would remember, later, that she hadn't gotten to seven.

Then she opened her eyes in the recovery room of a plastic-surgery clinic on the western edge of Montreal, not all at once but in stages, emerging from unconsciousness, then diving back like a dolphin playing in water. She'd been carried to a room where flowers were waiting for her: lilacs, orchids, red roses, two large pillows, and a new blanket where a note from Marc Gagnon awaited her, though she hadn't been able to read it yet.

The operation lasted many hours, softened by the death that general anaesthesia brings, where the sensation of time does not exist. Not only had she kept no memory of it, but she felt as though she hadn't lived through it at all. A period of her life had been removed from her memory, deleted, then two disparate moments were stuck back together.

She had pain between her legs like a drum beating its rhythm deep inside her, but the pain was eased by the morphine cradling her, she was suckling on it, like a thumb, a bottle that provided comfort. When the morphine ran out, the drum beat harder. The pain was intense and reassured her: what had to be done had been done, and done well. The walls of her vagina had been tightened with lasers, her inner lips made smaller and the hood covering her clitoris had been pulled back to reveal it, to thrust into the open the pink teat of her pussy forever alert, a pressure-point seeking caresses, a splinter.

Her pussy had become the Ideal Pussy. Charles could lick it, nibble on it, pinch it, fuck it, but more than anything photograph it and place it in his collection. Her Pussy might travel the Internet, why not, creep into the lives of other men and push away their women. In her bed with its thick covers where she was all but buried, a new idea formed: she would give herself to Charles, but to all men as well.

At age thirty, it was late to be a woman but, still, not too late. She still had five years, maybe ten, to reign over men's desires before losing her crown forever.

When the pain overwhelmed her, Rose rang and the morphine returned, entering her veins thanks to a nurse who arrived at the press of a button, whose face showed that she knew the nature of her operation, and that nature disgusted her.

Jealous, Rose thought, like all the others. She often wondered whether women who worked in this business were tempted to have surgery, or whether they were disgusted by it, like accountants with bills to pay.

Deep inside, she didn't care. With her Pussy, she wouldn't need to care about other women, that torment of always feeling out of place was finally over. These bits of skin that had been taken off made her part of the world, no matter what the world thought. Through her new-found tightness, her pussy like a tireless erection, Rose would give pleasure to Charles but to others as well. She would take her place among them and it would be a place she built for herself, that hadn't been given to her, it was a long path and she had walked it.

She woke from the operation with the belief that her life would change, and now she had to work on that conviction, the same way her pussy had been worked on.

For the first time she thought of Renald and Stéphane, her father and her brother, like men. She wanted to talk to them, and open herself up to them. Ideas came calmly to her, strung together without conflict, they didn't contain the weight of abomination that had thrown her onto a bench a month earlier.

One of the visual ideas that came to her was the image of a strip joint where she was dancing on stage, she saw herself being watched by a crowd of men. There was the club where she was dancing nude but also the magazines where her photos ran, always naked, legs spread, she thought of the men who would buy the magazines and be in thrall of her pussy that recalled the days before hair sullied sex, the cleanliness of the time before menstruation, almost pubescent but already expert. The transsexual she'd seen in Marc's waiting room came to mind, she saw him in the burden of the wrong body, like a low blow from nature, inspiring sympathy in Rose that comforted her.

Rose had surrendered and her surrender was like giving birth. Through her Pussy, she'd given herself life.

When the morphine faded completely, the pain neared an intolerable level and Rose rang, the door to her room opened and the morphine came in accompanied by the nurse who said nothing, who barely looked at her, asked nothing of her, except to describe her pain on a scale from one to ten to determine the dose.

At one point Marc entered the room and sat next to the bed. He took back the note he had written: "*I love you, Rose. Be better now. Let's be good together. Marc.*"

That love letter was clearly ridiculous, he said to himself as he watched Rose sleep. In some situations love should be taboo, and kept at a distance, he thought. Unlike Rose, he wasn't too sure about what he'd done, he regretted it already. He loved what she had before, her comforting folds, and gazing upon the ablation he'd committed, with the sutures and what he imagined would be the results, one thing was clear: Rose was no longer completely Rose. The illusion of her fragile size, the way he could grab her and hold her, that could hold no longer. Rose was impressive in her will, she couldn't be small, the whole time she was the one who led. She convinced him to undertake this operation, and he could never possess her.

"Rose? I'm here. When you're ready, we'll go home. It's better if you're at my house. I have everything we need to take care of you."

"Thanks, Marc. Thanks a lot," Rose said, not looking at him, with the ecstatic appearance of a woman who has just deposited in a priest's ear, on her deathbed, the poisonous sin long held hidden.

Her gratitude hurt him. What was she thanking him for? He wanted to lie next to her and hold her, better, to understand her, her and what she'd been looking for, what she seemed to have found.

OUTSIDE, SPRING WAS filling the air, everything was in warmth. In Westmount with its streets lined with trees and children, passersby, not young careerists like on the Plateau, but established professionals, parents, Westmount was full of parks, restaurants, and cafés, steep streets with increasingly luxurious houses. The closer you got to the top of the mountain, the more the world smelled like paradise, at least if you were Marc Gagnon's age. The reedy sound of nature found space to resonate and expand, contrary to downtown Montreal where pigeons cooed in traffic and showered cars and streets with their shit, the sidewalks blocked by the homeless who wandered with plastic bags filled with other plastic bags, sometimes surrounded by huge dogs. Compared to downtown where nature was made of pigeons, dogs, and the homeless all after the same crumbs, a family ecosystem searching for something to eat, empty bottles and cigarette butts, compared to that, Westmount smelled good.

Rose and Marc were walking side by side down Sherbrooke West, in the sweet air.

A month had gone by since the operation, a month of euphoria but anxiety too, for deep movements continued to excite and move through Rose. Since her vaginoplasty, she often had the impression that she'd been stabbed from the inside. She would suffer vertigo at the idea that none of this was necessary, it was a bad joke, *auto-da-fé* in the name of an image she had come upon one night, formed by the words Marc had spoken about a patient of his. During that month she found the time to surf the Internet and located a site she visited every time she felt unsure. It was the website of a Belgian clinic: "*Most patients are very happy after a decrease in the size of the labia and a tightening of the vagina. Often they regret not having done the operation far earlier. The comfort and self-esteem substantially increase the quality of their lives."*

"Happy. Far earlier. Increase the quality of their lives." Rose said the words out loud, in front of the screen, like a prayer.

Rose gained confidence as she read further passages: "*Sexual satisfaction is directly related to the increase in friction.*"

"Will I be normal?"

She often asked the question, and always received the same answer: "Yes. You'll be different but normal. I promise."

She saw Charles again and had been worried. He wasn't the same, he'd lost his photographer's eye. When she asked him questions about his projects, he hesitated, his eyes averted, scanning the room in short bursts as if tracking a fly, though more often than not he stared right above her forehead, though never more than a second or two. He told her he wasn't with Julie anymore but he hadn't tried to approach Rose, even though she'd asked him to.

"I missed you," he admitted. "I wanted to call you but I didn't have your number."

This news of the separation should have cheered Rose, but she felt the rug had been pulled from under her feet. She couldn't let weakness show, when she conquered Charles again, Charles would get better. He was tired, his shoulders slumped forward, everything about him was duller, down to his hair that had lost its shine, but Rose didn't notice the changes until the end of her visit. She never really looked at men, her eyes couldn't take them in. That'll have to change, she told herself, feeling Charles' distress but not knowing what to do about it.

But the meeting had its upside.

"You look good," he allowed, and as they kissed goodbye, his eyes gained their photographer's focus, and he held her in his arms, letting her go on a strong note.

The Ideal Pussy that had lost some of its power in her mind after so many manifestations of pain and itching, so many bandages, was beginning to heal. The stitches had dissolved, the red and yellow discharges had become rarer, the swelling was easing. Though it didn't yet look like anything known by man, it was beginning to show signs of health, it would soon be ready to act. The night before, she telephoned Julie who'd been waiting for her call. The shoot was to take place the next Saturday on the roof of the building, the date had been set. In anticipation, Julie distributed leaflets to the building's residents to announce they wouldn't have access to the roof that day: *Photo shoot Saturday, July 22, between 12:00 and 4:00 pm*, she'd written in bold.

Charles was ready, Julie said, she was ready to roll, she claimed, because of the documentary project that she *felt*.

"Rose! I'm happy you called me. If you want, we can see each other and talk ahead of time about...well, the whole story."

"Nothing to say. You and I will never be a team."

In the past month, life had brought so many surprises, and they went against her plans. She thought she would steal Charles away from Julie, but wouldn't need to in the end; she believed she'd fight Julie sodden with drink, but now she'd have to face a different adversary.

"I agreed to do this for Charles. I've begun working for him again, every so often, but not like before. I have other important projects that don't concern you."

"That's fine with me. But Charles isn't feeling right. You must know that. You must have seen it. I want to talk to you about that. He might need our help."

Our help, she'd said. *Bitch*.

"If he's not doing well, it's because of you."

There was a silence at the other end of the line that told Rose her aim was true.

Walking on Sherbrooke West, Marc put one hand on Rose's shoulder, making them a couple in the eyes of human convention and the passersby who looked at them like one, a real one. But their looks didn't bother Rose, on the contrary, never again, she liked to imagine, would she be seen other than with a man.

They sat on a park bench like a comfortable couple that needs few words, that can guess each other's thoughts. The sunlight poured down upon the trees whose leaves filtered dancing diamonds here and there upon them, but this affluent tranquility, the bourgeois quality of the environment that expelled poverty from its sphere, was far from Rose's mind. She pictured herself on the roof of the building, in Charles' studio where she would pose for him, in other places too, that they'd never gone to but that she'd heard about, like so many Ali Baba caverns where she would luxuriate, she believed, or at least not have to fight anymore.

Rose was already back on her planet of fashion, photos, runways. If she had to be a servant, she would serve men and not women.

"When I start making money again, I'm going to live in my own apartment. Alone."

Marc Gagnon was caught in the trap of youth. He'd known from the start that he could not possess it, unless he hid from the fact that he wasn't loved, something he was entirely capable of.

"You won't be my patient anymore. And I'm not trying to blackmail you."

"Yes, I will be," she answered. "I want to. I'm your mistress and I will be as long as you want me. Sincerely."

Marc looked into the distance where earth and sky met, where the forces that move the world begin, waiting to be freed, making the world turn despite human will. He couldn't help feeling relieved at what he'd heard.

"You do me a lot of good," she went on. "If you fall in love with another woman, it'll be something else entirely. I'll let you be."

"Are you still in love with Charles?"

Rose didn't answer. At least, Marc thought, she isn't lying. He thought of his wife whom he missed sometimes, and whom he'd started seeing from a different point of view. Since Rose had come into his life, he'd been sad with that vague sadness that accompanies the awareness of times passed. But he would keep Rose and the sadness that came with her, because despite the operation that had cracked her open and taken from her whatever virginity she still had, he still wanted her at his side, he couldn't help himself.

A little boy who'd been jumping up and down on a picnic table began running in circles, shouting war cries, to the great pleasure of his sister watching him and clapping in encouragement. In his widening circles, he moved closer to the sidewalk where people were walking, then closer to the traffic. His mother got up from the bench where she was keeping watch over them, dropping her book.

"François! François!"

The child started sprinting down the sidewalk in the triumph of boyhood, cutting past the passersby who parted to let him go. His mother began to panic, she ran after him, yelling,

"François! Stop! Stay there, François! Stop!" But François loved the idea of a chase, the hunt was on and he was the prey, he ran ever faster, letting out a constant high-pitched cry, beautiful, almost a chant. Then his mother understood that she would cause the worst possible outcome, she changed her tone, now she was shrieking, "Françoooooois! Stooop! Stooop! Stooop!" The game wasn't funny anymore, and the boy halted in midstride. He watched his mother run toward him, he didn't know what to do, he was already beginning to apologize with his posture, the way he put his hands in his pockets, almost ashamed. Once she'd caught the child, she fell on her knees and burst into tears, trapping him in her arms like a wild beast.

Poor mother, poor child, Rose lamented, thinking of the quantity of tears this woman would shed for her boy, and the indecent weight of those tears on him; he would have to take measures to protect himself from this great fear of the world unless he wanted to live like a drowning man.

After they watched the mother crying over her child, the couple returned to Marc's house.

"Why don't we go out and eat at Chez L'Épicier tonight?"

"Good idea," he replied, taking her by the waist and guiding her upstairs.

In the bedroom, Rose gave Marc the only part of her she could: her mouth. She worked his cock the way you watch a dish in the oven: calmly, mind elsewhere, without pleasure or disgust, with gratitude for this man who never sought to come between her and her desires, who instead helped them along.

Later, in the bathroom as she was getting ready to go out, she looked at her pussy in a small mirror. A Jivaro doll. The inner lips had disappeared.

"For every woman, it should be natural to be able to show her body without shame, hang-ups, or fear."

Rose put the mirror back in her handbag and closed her eyes to concentrate on the conviction she'd woken up with after the operation, the one she had worked to keep alive.

There was still plenty to do.

JULIE O'BRIEN WAS jogging outside, earphones on, "Under my Thumb" blaring, a Rolling Stones song in the warm air of July. She was making her way toward the Mountain that she would scale then go back down to Java U, where she'd write for a few hours, relaxing in front of a tuna sandwich, why not, and a glass of carrot juice.

While running up the mountain on the Mount Royal Avenue side, she saw Charles. He was sitting on a bench, easily recognizable with his fashionable haircut, wavy, golden locks upon his head, a metrosexual haircut, or was that ubersexual, it depended on your point of view. He was looking straight ahead as if in deep meditation. Julie ran toward him, realizing as she slowed down how hard she'd pushed herself.

To try and catch her breath, she leaned against the bench, but her wind escaped her so she unhooked a water bottle from her belt, hoping that the drink would calm her. Charles was concentrating on whatever it was he was looking at, and hadn't detected her presence, his mind had left his body and was travelling through memory where the world was falling apart in a way he could not comprehend. The order of things was broken, his head was a pool table where the triangle of numbered balls was broken by the cue ball, it seemed to him it kept on breaking over and over again, shooting the balls toward the four corners of the table in a thunder of collision and destruction.

"Charles? How are you?"

Charles turned toward her but his eyes seemed unable to focus on her. Then, as recognition loomed, he jolted backward.

"Charles?" she repeated, leaning over him slightly.

"You, here? You were looking for me? You followed me?"

"No, I saw you by accident. With the good weather I've been running on the Mountain more often. Why?"

Julie sat next to him and Charles calmed down a little. His beautiful full lips searched for words, while the mouth in his three-day beard produced no sound.

"What's happening? You're scaring me."

"You sent me those pictures over the Internet?"

"Pictures? No, I haven't sent you anything."

"Strange. I was sure it was you. To make me understand how sick I am. To punish me."

The traffic was dense on Park Avenue, techno music poured from a convertible with the roof down, four teenage boys scanned the sidewalk for girls eager to show off their booty.

"It wasn't me. I swear, I'm not trying to punish you. I never wanted to punish you. I just wanted..."

Julie didn't know what to say, it was clear she had often wanted to punish him, and they both knew it.

"I got some pictures. Weird ones. I don't know who sent them to me. Someone who knows me, for sure."

"Pictures of what?"

Charles went silent and put his head down.

"Porn?"

"Yes. Well, I guess."

"Maybe they were sent automatically, to promote a site you visited. Have you thought of that?"

"No, that's not it. They were taken for me, with a goal in mind. But it'll be okay, it'll be okay."

"Listen. I put a lot of pressure on you for the shoot Saturday, but if you don't want to, we can forget it. No problem."

Charles rubbed his face with his hand, then looked at his watch that was at eye level.

"Maybe you need to get out of the world of photography and images, at least for a while. Maybe the proximity to bodies…"

"No," Charles interrupted. "It's the opposite."

Charles was smiling now, but his smile was fragile. When Julie tried to stroke the back of his neck with her hand, he twisted away from her again, as if facing a dentist's needle aimed straight at his open mouth.

The conversation was over, and Julie resumed her run without pushing it. She knew that by pushing too hard, she'd gotten Charles into a place where she couldn't reach him. For her as well, life was an endless battle, a world without war or mass graves, where the horrors of the globe were a pitch in a marketing meeting for the United Colors of Benetton, where misery and famine were mostly seen at the box office, where the bloody reality of countries destroyed by armed conflict could be digested in the expression of your personal opinion, but her world without war or mass graves was still, when you looked closely and carefully, full of shit.

Without knowing it, men had fought for this world of freedom, this life of endless choices; the massacres of the past had led to these lives that held no danger, except perhaps from yourself, and now, as you stepped over the slaughter of History, you could despair about your own life. But everyone had his cross to bear, a dead god on his back, the saviour's corpse, Julie thought. For now, her only care was to scale the Mountain that, like everyone else, wore a cross at its peak, a fossil, the vestige which said that somewhere near here, a god had lived.

EARLIER THAT MORNING, Charles Nadeau had made his way to the studio like every other morning to select and touch up the photos of a sixteen-year-old model, a breathtaking beauty, though inexperienced. She would be the cover of *Elle Québec* for the month of September, the most popular edition of the year. In the host of pictures he would find a few good ones, but he knew, even without looking at them, that most had been spoiled by the model's reflexes. Despite his warnings and recommendations to remain natural, and without any particular intention, she had pushed her lips forward like a kiss and narrowed her eyes, believing, no doubt, that she was giving added strength to her look. Models, in their poses, were often preceded by horrendous clichés.

The previous day's shoot had tired him more than usual, and he still hadn't quite gotten his energy back. That morning, he'd felt oppressed by the extraordinary number of people walking every which way, coming toward him with their magnetized lives, despite it being so early. The material existence of other Montrealers was intolerable, impossible to escape, as if each body that passed raped his own.

On the screen in his dark studio, he examined hundreds of photos and felt, after half an hour, as disgusted and impotent as he had when looking at the pornographic images in his repertoire which he had since erased.

Yet the two couldn't be more unlike each other in Charles' eyes. The model was wearing a series of white dresses, and everything had been whitewashed, cleaned, with no possible entry, and Charles couldn't see the link between the virginal, impeccable body of the model and the brutality of what got him hard. There was something foul about moving from pornography to fashion, like a bacteria; the results of the shoot were contaminated by his new point of view on them, a gift of clairvoyance that revealed the rot despite the appearance of the pictures, despite their decency. Julie would have said she'd added that word to his vocabulary—decency—just for him. Something had changed in those pictures that were decomposing before his eyes, he could make out a swarm, seething activity, yet still indefinable.

On first inspection everything seemed normal, the young model looked like a bride in a fluffy wedding gown, but things didn't stay so simple for long. Charles dug deeper than the surface, revealing that this beauty was metal-plated, gold leaf over a bloody background, a flowery shroud that hid crude flesh and its organic workings. It was as if the cleanliness of the photos revealed, in the limpidness of the model's skin, in her dense grain, carefully made up, in the purity of her young body, what this body would become and what it already was: an inanimate, putrid thing. Her smooth, hermetic adolescent body, that once would have comforted him, now threatened, loomed. Her seamless beauty seemed about to fall apart. It shocked him, and his own body reacted with discomforting sensations: muscle pains and headaches, an almost perpetual state of fatigue.

Despite that feeling, he worked for more than two hours. His sight gained further acuity through the exercise, and it kept advancing the borders beyond which the body no longer existed.

He returned to pictures he'd worked on in the past, a few years ago. They too were contaminated. All these pictures that had once given off light, that had been filled with a soft wind of beauty, like fairies landing on a silvery veil over the darkness, now revealed a hidden face, and wore a death mask. Before his eyes, the skin peeled off and showed what lay beneath: injured flesh under alluring pouts, come-hither looks, open, rouged lips, cute curls cascading onto bare shoulders, long legs, juvenile bodies with no fat, both bony and soft, true models.

Death was there at the heart of beauty, and his own body, faced with death, pulled back, found ways to turn away, whether he was sitting or not, in front of his computer. His thoughts followed the same movement toward shapelessness, lost in troubled water, muddy bottoms, and the end of life, the genesis of which took the form of messages sent to him. But what was he being told?

He managed to choose the best photos of the young model, a dozen or so, but then he had to penetrate them with his cursor and move over them to touch them up. He knew this would be the worst part: as he zoomed in on various parts to fix them, the whole disappeared and the parts emerged, magnifying skin that didn't look like skin anymore. He was moving into a place never before seen that vomited marine creatures from the deepest abyss where no light had ever shone before that instant. As he feared, every dilated pore, every fine line on her skin, every blemish and red vein at the corner of her eyes seemed like an infringement to him, spittle sticky like a foretaste of the tomb.

A little before eleven o'clock, he left the studio to get some fresh air, walked briskly toward Pine Avenue and, without forethought, entered a hair salon. The shampoo did him good, but when he sat in front of the mirror, in front of his own image, he felt that same feeling of disintegration, that same toothless face behind his own. He couldn't follow the flow of words from the hairdresser; the face in the mirror belonged to another. He closed his eyes, communicating to the hairdresser that he was overworked, a passing thing, probably just the beginning of a cold.

He found the energy to return to his studio and finish his work, having had the time to take a long detour all the way to the Mountain and then Saint Lawrence Boulevard, all the while reasoning with himself that his face couldn't be any other face but his. The photos were only just photos, after all, they couldn't be signs from hell meant for him to decipher.

Throwing the last of his strength into his work, he was as productive as usual, controlling his sight and forcing himself to consider only the surfaces of images likely to be looked at. But an event broke down his resistance, this time for good, and from then on he would never be able to doubt that there was a hidden program of destruction lurking behind his life, and the lives of all others.

A message from an anonymous email address arrived with the usual brief *ping* in his inbox, the address he almost never used, and gave only to those close to him. He didn't recognize the sender's address, and was about to delete it without reading it, but the subject line attracted him: *Something to be licked.*

"THIS IS WHAT I WILL SOON OFFER YOU, IN PLEASURE AND WITH LOVE," he read. There was no signature.

The pictures were an open mouth, they were what was vomiting and what was vomited. It was the inside of a body, he figured, in any case, something human.

He explored the details as he had with the young model's photos, without understanding what he was looking at. But his heart was beating and his lungs were compressed, he felt his being desert him, trying to escape what the screen was forcing on him. In one of the pictures, he saw something he recognized: two fingers, two fake nails, a French manicure, exploring the middle where there was an opening. In the last picture, a finger entered the hole, and the manicured nail was lost from view.

Charles could barely swallow; he had understood what he was seeing. A woman's genitals. He'd seen the same thing on the Internet, but now he could not keep his eyes in check, he saw the surfaces folded over themselves like a pair of gloves. It was a naked pussy that had no more skin because death had taken it for itself, a pussy like a path open to him, a hidden message. Through this pussy he would discover what was expected of him, and what had been trying to come to the surface for some time now. The pussy on the screen was about to open its mouth and say something important, but Charles wasn't ready to hear it, he turned his head away, his strength left him and he could not face the unbelievable object that showed itself to him in such dramatic fashion, impossible to avoid since that morning.

Outside again, he wandered a second time toward the Mountain to try and make sense of his thoughts. There, he met Julie. Obviously she was behind the pictures, who else could it be?

Returning home, a constant buzz filled his head and broke his last link with the world. The swarming of pictures into decomposition had moved into him, into his mind where his new-found gift of clairvoyance lay. It continued haunting him to make sure he could hear its uproar.

X

THE SHOOT

IT WAS A GORGEOUS DAY. The sky, uniformly blue, was pure and cloudless, except in the distance, if you looked close enough, over the Jacques Cartier Bridge, small rips of cotton, tender clusters just over the horizon. The sun was low and strong, yet delicate and discreet, a ball of light that kept its distance, tied to the Earth by an invisible wire. It was only eleven o'clock in the morning, but summer was alive and golden, August was approaching quickly, Julie feared, hell had waltzed into Montreal to open wide the doors to its oven, at least until autumn.

Julie noticed that the guardrail had been repaired. She tested it and it had swayed; shoddy work. To be careful, she placed the picnic tables and the bottle-green parasols to block the path to the guardrail, unless you made an effort to climb over them.

She'd spent the previous day making food to feed the crew both during and after the shoot that would be a kind of celebration. She made sandwiches of all sorts, with cold cuts and grilled vegetables, and potato and chickpea salad. She also bought a dozen bottles of flat and sparkling water, two litres of orange juice, grenadine syrup, lemons and cherries and, of course, to pay everyone for their efforts, eight bottles of champagne, two of which were already on the roof—Veuve Clicquot, to be drunk after four o'clock in the afternoon, at least by her, and while eating, and out of the sun's glare. The reserves were kept in the shade, at the edge of the deck, in two large containers filled with ice that she would replenish if need be.

She had organized everything with unusual effort, surprising even to her. Perhaps, she thought, she didn't need to love to live, maybe the best way to live was without love.

At first, there would be only her, Rose, and Charles, four hours for a photo shoot, giving Julie time to define the perfect angle to capture their bodies. André and Bertrand would join them at 4:00 PM giving them enough time to review the pictures that Charles would transfer onto his laptop equipped with a high-speed connection even on the roof. The rest of the day would follow the particular inspiration that came to them; either everyone would go home or continue to celebrate there on the roof, inviting the building's residents to join them. Olivier Blanchette, the cameraman with whom she'd worked during *Children for Adults Only*, would come and film the shoot. He would stay for the party. Julie was sure he could wrap his head around the concept.

Her body was lightly tanned and her muscles scarcely defined, but she was slowly getting back into shape, her relapse now seemed to be part of a distant past, a bad patch experienced by someone else, a story she heard. As she got older, the distance between her and her memories lengthened. They fell away from her like a book she'd read a long time ago, then forgotten.

She was leaning against the guardrail, but far from where the lightning had struck, sunscreen on her shoulders speckled with clusters of freckles. Her left shoulder had healed, though when she was tired or lifted heavy weights, her injury awoke in warm, rough waves, almost sensual.

Rose was first to arrive. Without making any noise, she surprised Julie who was lost in her thoughts like the first time they'd spoken to each other, one year before on the same roof, during the World Cup.

"How are you?" Rose said crisply, a coldness Julie decided not to attend to, to save herself the effort.

Julie had to raise her hand to shield her eyes from the sun that blinded her and hid Rose who, in this violent light, looked like an apparition. Rose moved closer, out of the sun's glare. The first thing Julie noticed was Rose's hair, as short as her own, or almost, a square cut that stopped at the chin, framing her face that seemed even younger, even more like a little girl than before. She was wearing a tight-fitting turquoise dress, platform shoes that showed her small feet with French-manicured nails, shoes that let her look Julie in the eyes since she was wearing flip-flops, her fuck-me shoes were stored next to the champagne, with the skimpy outfits just in case, and two bathing suits. Rose had paid for professional makeup, the real thing, her eyes were highlighted with deep, greyish-blue shadow, smoky eyes, but it had been done with good taste and skill, her eyebrows were darkened and raised with a pencil, her eyes seemingly wider, though that was an effect of Botox.

Over the past year, Rose had become more beautiful, but it was beauty from determined effort that spoke volumes about the time and money she'd invested. She had the vulva-body of the Madrid transsexuals, everything about her summoned up erections, her pussy covered her from head to toe like a leather skin. More than ever she was the perfect subject for a documentary, and Julie was glad about that.

"You look good. I can tell you're not wanting for money."

Julie immediately regretted her ironic tone. She was being rude and didn't know why. But at least rudeness was a kind of communication.

"I've had fortune in my misfortune, like they say," Rose answered in the same tone.

The blue sky, omnipresent and immense, was unmoving, like a still life. It would be perfect for the shoot, Rose calculated. She knew from experience that the sun, if she could use it, would serve her, as long as she could manipulate the shade created by the parasols and the array of spots and light boxes that Charles would bring, since she knew him by heart. But in the end, nothing else mattered more than when she felt so good, when she would return to Charles' eyes and stamp out Julie.

"I've started working with Charles again, but only on a contract basis."

"Really? Going back to school?"

Rose laughed a small bitter laugh, Julie eluded her again for some obscure reason, maybe she was jealous of this solid woman before her who remained strong despite failure, who hadn't been destroyed.

"Let's just say I'm reorienting my career. I'm changing things up. That's what a breakup will do for you. You get a new haircut, you do things you'd never have done before."

"You force him to stay, even if he's already gone."

"Things that go in the direction of the things loved by the one who left," she continued, ignoring Julie's last comment that she hadn't understood in any case.

"Things like what's going to happen today."

Silence fell between them as usual, as it always did when they weren't drunk, silence during which Rose moved toward the tables and the green umbrellas to look over at the guardrail, making no comment about the furniture.

"The situation is a little unreal," Julie admitted. "But it's completely spontaneous, and we can stop at any time."

Spontaneous? Not really, Rose told herself.

"It's unreal, but we're all unreal these days," Julie added, raising her voice so Rose could hear her as she walked among the tables.

"It's true. We live in an unreal world."

Rose walked around the deck slowly, stopping here and there, a doll looking into the distance that seemed not like a horizon but some cardboard background. She lifted her chin toward the world around her so the world might see her perched on her platform shoes, her back arched, running a hand through her hair.

Rose rifled through the sandwiches and bottles, and picked up Julie's black patent leather shoes, the kind you wore for an audience when dancing around a pole, and in the other hand she had a bottle of champagne. She straightened herself and held out her hands to Julie, a smile playing on her lips, a fake smile, drawing a parallel between the shoes and the champagne. With one easy movement she tossed the shoes back in the corner.

"Is the champagne for drinking now?" she said, pointing at the bottle. "May I?"

Julie felt a pinch in her stomach; an answer to Rose's question. She checked her watch, the torment readable on her face. Noon, and Charles still hadn't arrived.

"Do what you want. It's a bit early for me, though. Don't you think?"

Rose looked for the champagne glasses, found them, and set them out on a table. A minute later the cork flew with a *pop* and hit the inside of an umbrella, and Julie felt it had popped in her stomach, she tensed, trying to digest and expel it.

"I've got your girly cigarettes, Benson & Hedges Ultra Light King Size."

Julie looked at her glass overflowing with bubbles. Oh, well, she told herself, see you tomorrow. The two women clinked their glasses, cheers, and they drank to the shoot about to happen, cheers, and the future while they were at it, cheers.

"I have to tell you something before we can't talk about it," Julie began, placing her glass on the table. "Charles is in a state and he's trying to hide it. Since I'm tied to the way he is now, it's best if you offer your help and make the next move."

"What's happening? What sort of state?"

"I don't know," she answered, massaging her stomach to calm the pinch of anxiety. "He seems distressed. That's the least you could say."

"Charles and I didn't talk about those things, the past and all the traumas. We never talked about our families and what they'd done. Everything was always good between us. I never saw him feel bad two days in a row."

The two women were sitting across from each other, looking at one another without judgment for once. Julie lifted her glass toward the sky whose blue faded into the golden colour of champagne. The bubbles were rapidly climbing, demonic, as they fizzed, when you brought your glass to your ear, they made a *pshhh* sound, like a snake's forked tongue about to attack.

"It's something to do with his sexuality. Well, to do with his tastes, that you know about."

Partially hidden by the large sunglasses she'd set on her nose, Rose's face froze.

"What?"

"His thing stopped working."

It was the first time the two women mentioned his unusual sexuality. Rose lowered her eyes, she was thinking of the pictures she'd sent him two days earlier and that he certainly had seen.

"Stopped working? What do you mean?"

"Like a machine giving up. I think that when it stopped, something in his head broke too. That's all I know."

"When was the last time you saw him?"

"Two days ago. He was at his lowest."

Rose put an acrylic nail in her mouth, her thumbnail, and began chewing on it, staring at her glass. Her Pussy, well-behaved until then, awoke and began sending all sorts of sensations from within. It knows we're talking about it, she thought, the way a beast knows its master's intentions.

"He told me about some pornographic pictures that were sent to him by someone who knows him. He thought it was me. But I figure that since you're familiar with his…universe…his repertoire…"

Julie wanted to continue, but the door to the roof opened and Charles appeared, carrying three aluminum boxes by their handles.

Rose moved to take one.

"Two boxes left downstairs, at my place."

"You need help?"

"No, I'll be fine. But you can start taking the equipment out."

He looks better than the other day, Julie thought. He looks strange, Rose lamented, unable to think of anything else but what she'd done, the pictures she'd sent, and what Julie had just said.

From out of the boxes, Rose took out a camera, a Nikon F5, lenses, filters, a tripod, a few lights, and umbrellas, and set them near a table where she would assemble it all, in the shade. She busied herself to hide from Julie, who was observing her, already in her role of scriptwriter, analyzing her subject, feeling that Rose was overwhelmed by the situation.

Then Olivier Blanchette showed up with his camera, followed by Charles who didn't know he was coming, and who didn't like having a cameraman.

THE SHOOT WAS about to start. Olivier was ready to film the scene. Julie had prepared the shoot, to Rose's disappointment, who imagined herself like a model in a photograph, made-up, sexy, varnished, and not like a sideshow, self-alienated, a hysteric behind bars. Her conviction, she reminded herself, must be her only commandment. She just had to think of the hidden reason for why she was on the roof, without which she would have never played this game, and her enthusiasm returned. It would be foolish to miss out on an opportunity she'd been dreaming of for so long, the way she'd destroy them both with the weapon between her legs. But life, as always, would not go according to her predictions, cunning bitch that she was.

The theme of the shoot demanded that the women be photographed without posing, captured by surprise, drinking champagne, eating, moving around, talking among themselves or on the phone, while ensuring that the plastic aspect of their bodies was in focus. That's where Charles' talent entered. He would have to shine his light on the well-planned aspect of their natural look, and not improve them too much with his storehouse of effects, his spots that lit and embellished, his filters that hid the irregularities of their skin—or so ran Julie's theory—she was talking too much, explaining too much, blathering on, which enraged Rose, but she had to keep quiet since she was part of the project, it was her plan, she'd consented to it after all, her vision of women buried under their pussies like quicksand. Rose like Rosine again, despite her Pussy that, in one hour or two, maybe three, would jump out like a jack-in-the-box.

Charles didn't say much, the project wasn't very complex except for the cameraman, but he learned to ignore Olivier after a while. He was calm, and completely in the moment, surprising when he considered that two days had passed since the events in his studio—where he hadn't returned since, fearing that the experience might return. He understood what Julie was trying to do, having listened to her many times on the subject, thankfully the sun's glare on their bodies hid them in a halo of light that kept him from sensing his vile clairvoyance, his third eye that dug graves. The wind, the noise around him, the movement of both women playing their parts as if nothing was happening at all—Julie perfectly embodying the role while Rose had difficulty not posing—prevented them from puking themselves up on his lens. Their environment made them airtight, the sky, the sun, and the air locked them into their bodies, set down a protective filter between him and them.

Both women were eating, mostly Julie who wanted to put off the time when she wouldn't be able to stop drinking. Sometimes she put on one of her bathing suits, only to realize that her body no longer had anything special; time had rounded her belly that had never had the chance to bear life, the skin of her ass was striped with small stretch marks and had loosened a little, despite her efforts, not to mention the scars left by the razor blades, small fine lines, white or pink, that covered her breasts and the inside of her thighs, lines like scratches that would fade with time, but which, for now, couldn't pass unseen. So be it, Julie thought, another preoccupation that she would have to forget about like a sentence passed, left to age in peace, as her memories already had. Rose missed nothing of the changes in Julie's body, and found herself magnificent by comparison. She prided herself at being younger even if it was only by three years, she congratulated herself at finally being one of the winners, one of those women who make men fall on their knees, who see every door in their path open, letting them walk toward new doors that will also soon open, in a perpetual parade where obstacles disappear by themselves, one after the other.

The shoot was taking place in a calm atmosphere; an outside observer would have been bored. Olivier kept a safe distance, zooming in sometimes on Charles, sometimes on Julie, but most often on Rose, who was showing off. It was hotter than forecast. In the blue sky the sun had grown larger, swollen with itself, satisfied, bringing with it water vapour that appeared on the horizon, small white stringy clouds like cotton candy, Julie imagined, sensitive to the emerging effects of alcohol that brightened her, made her childish.

"Julie! Don't you have more champagne at your place? I thought I heard you say that."

"Yes, but be careful, the sun hits hard when you drink. No need to rush, anyway."

Julie the drunk dispensed hygienic advice that, for once, she was able to follow, probably because she'd promised herself, once the shoot was done, once the pictures had been reviewed and filed away, to really let go, and drink to the dregs, until she lost herself, the way she wanted. Especially since André would be joining them soon, in a couple of hours at most, with some "wake-up," the euphemism he had found for cocaine, that white vixen who would give her a second wind.

Still in her platform shoes, Rose was playing her new character; she's changed, Charles and Julie both observed without consulting each other, exchanging conspiratorial looks when Rose went too far and became almost comical, with her serious, almost solemn air. She'd taken off the top of her dress and pulled it down over her belly button that she'd pierced and fitted with a small white diamond. She was covering her body with cream, not to protect herself from the sun, but for the cream effect, using it to caress herself in front of Charles. Not only was he not amused, but he waited for her to stop to photograph the moment when she lost patience, a game that angered her.

"You're a terrible model," he said.

Nothing could have annoyed her more, and because he resisted her attempts to attract him, she would later remember, she took the fatal decision to publicly humiliate him, forcing him into a corner.

"Look who's talking! You don't think I don't know what you usually ask of your models?"

"That's not what I'm saying. Being a good model means following directions, and the direction here is to be photographed outside of a pose. You're annoyed, and that's what's interesting, we need to exploit it."

"I accept more than you think. And annoyance can't be

exploited, the way you say. If you do exploit it, then it's still a game, it's still a pose."

Rose got up and grabbed a bottle of champagne that Julie had just set in the ice bucket. Too hurried to open it, she hadn't taken the time to tear off the gold paper that covered the neck, and hadn't been able to pop the cork. As she tried to open the bottle that wouldn't comply, she hurt her thumb and broke a nail.

"Fuck! Fuck!"

For the first time that day, Charles actually enjoyed looking at her. He seized the moment and started shooting away, moving in closer on her.

"Stop! Shit, stop!"

"You're too serious, Rose. Have some fun," he said, aiming his camera at her until he got too close and she ripped it from his hands, the way a child takes another child's toy away from him, not to play with it, but simply to take it away.

"You're not funny. Why are you doing this to me? No woman wants to lose control over her image, so no woman can play this game of yours. How can you not know this? You, the great photographer, the bitch-maker."

Charles couldn't believe it. Rose had never talked to him that way, with those words. *Lose control. Bitch-maker.* With her words, he remembered the porn pictures he'd received, pussy sent from an unknown email address. The pictures jostled inside him; he still had that anxiety of meat, of sequestration and his father's insanity. But the anxiety vanished because he'd just realized a truth: all of it, everything that had occurred and would occur, everything that life had been so far with its suit of trials, had been indispensable. Rose had illuminated him.

His life was part of a project bigger than he was, a necessary project in which he played a central role. The project was that of the Will.

It's her, he'd understood. Will has placed her on my path.

He saw the pussy on his screen at the same time he saw himself in Pierre's house, his father's house, sitting in front of a plate heaped with meat and potatoes that made him nauseous as Pierre told him the story of the female creatures that have an eye inside their pussy. All of it, the pussy pictures that he now attributed to Rose, his clairvoyance that saw under the skin, and his father's story about the Amazons' pussy-eye, was beginning to take form in his mind, revealing its narrative logic. Ideas were emerging from obscurity to appear in the light of day and be confirmed as revelation, sent to him through signs that carried an important message, signs from another world, that of the dead, of lost souls. His father could be attempting to speak to him.

Rose noticed Charles' disturbed look. She calmed down and gave him back his camera.

"Julie told me you weren't doing so well. You can talk to me if you want. She said she'd caused you harm."

"You women. Always talking."

He put away his camera in a box, then sat in the shadow cast by one of the umbrellas. He lit a cigarette to relax, but the buzzing that had filled his head in the studio a few days earlier awoke in him again, gaining in intensity with each passing second, becoming liquid frenzy, as if he were standing near a roiling sea. Soon Charles could hear the crashing waves, his mind was being pulled this way and that by great swells of water that threw themselves at the cliff's bottom where they broke, white explosions covering steel grey, a repeating percussion of wave, break, wave, break, the cliffs shuddering. He could see Rose and Julie through the din of water splitting against the rocks, he observed them without being part of what they were, or in the place where they were; they existed on a plane where he no longer belonged.

"I'm going to stop for a second, I've got to catch my breath."

"I can transfer the pictures to your laptop, if you want." Julie suggested.

"I'll do that by myself, downstairs, alone and quiet."

Charles left the roof. Julie went on eating, drinking, and smoking, she had passed a point of no return, she could feel joy in her heart, a celebration, love to give, she was trying in vain to start a conversation with Rose who was disgusted and starting to feel a little drunk, trying to remain steadfast in her belief, and in her treasure that had not yet been revealed. She stopped trying to pull her dress down, it had climbed up and was revealing her ass: two round, tanned cheeks that had swallowed a white satin G-string, which Olivier couldn't help filming.

"I've got a friend I want to introduce you to," Julie suggested. "He'll be here soon."

"He's into women, at least?"

"Yes. And generally they can't resist him."

Rose smiled, sadness apparent under her façade.

"By the way," Julie continued, "I looked up the statistics of births by gender. You're completely wrong."

"I don't care."

"So why'd you tell me what you told me?"

Julie and Rose looked at each other and smiled through the vapours of alcohol, in it they saw the confused dance of memories from the previous months, both pathetic and terrible. All of that had been pretty serious, pretty ceremonious, for not much return, Julie thought, as Rose, who had a hand on her pussy under the table, was slowly getting herself off with Olivier secretly filming from the next table. He was filming Rose who knew she was being filmed and had stopped right before coming. It's working, it's working, she told herself, reassured. Soon it'll be time.

CHARLES WAS IN his loft, blinds drawn against the midday sun that warmed the city, now overexposed, victim of the sun's implacable rays.

The crashing waves had changed into a muted, throbbing background, like the hum of a high-tension line. On his computer screen, he examined the results of the shoot that had reawakened his clairvoyance. Something had changed since the studio; the movement had become clearer, images gained in texture, in thickness, bodies moved freely and with more volume, almost elegantly, as if they had been made from worms that had joined with the skin, twisting and turning in quivering, self-regulated life. But this time, he knew, the foresight he had acquired wasn't accidental or temporary, it wasn't a threat either, quite the opposite, it was a door open to the Truth, a gift from the Will that carried him further than other people, all of whom were blind and without his gift. He was far superior to them, with a gift that still didn't have a name, that made him the most important man in the world, and the loneliest one as well. The price to pay: solitude and the incomprehension of others, he would gladly pay.

He was the first man on earth, the second, rather, after his father, to see what he saw. Flesh was no longer anxiety-inducing or even pleasure-inducing, but real, simply real, it existed in the world, bordered humans, but also boiled over into a sort of elsewhere. But nobody could see this, except him. Through the pictures, he could read encoded messages that revealed keys to him, and these messages spoke of a global threat, obscure, the nature of which needed to be defined but certainly spoke of a foreign power that would annihilate man.

He travelled through the photos. The faster he scrolled through them, the more Rose, attempting to undress and reveal something to him, a secret, his mission, showed her anger. Her face that was set against a turbulent sky, like any sky painted by Van Gogh, filled with long, sinuous, serpentine shapes, telling of a fury that was not only hers, but of the Will too. In a few pictures, too few pictures, he could see her ass, half uncovered, that suggested an opening, that undulated in the movement that turned on itself to swallow itself up. A tanned ass that invited forceful entry through the white satin of the G-string on which the light was reflected, like a star in a smile, an invitation to which he hadn't submitted, since he was still a blind man.

Then a voice in his mind, no doubt his father's, the prime messenger of the Will, spoke:

"She gave you a sign, and you didn't follow it."

Charles wasn't afraid, he was ready. The voice came at the right moment, confirming his intuitions. It gave logical meaning, and a salutary one, to the dreadful transformations the world had undergone over the past few weeks. Never had things been clearer: he had entered a new world that opened itself for him so that he might capture Truth, this world had chosen him.

"When she returns, be guided by this voice."

Charles opened the pictures of Rose's pussy as wide as he could get them. They now inspired in him nothing but awe and incomparable respect, an urgent desire to read them too, and decode the message, a desire to remain alert and concentrated until their truth was revealed. His entire life, he knew now, had converged toward this pussy, his whole life had been waiting for it. The movement of the worms over the pussy was slower and deeper still, everything moved in circular, hypnotic fashion.

The time that passed seemed like an eternity, but nothing needed to be rushed. He was discovering God, and God was his Father. His butcher shop, his meat, was only a façade before Truth that Pierre had tried to transmit to him, though he hadn't been ready to hear it at the time.

The movement traced patterns that were becoming more precise. In the middle of the flesh an eye opened, not the image of an eye, not a photographed eye, but a real one, a living eye that moved, its pupil scanning in every direction as if to ensure that no one, except Charles, was in the room. After a moment, the eye looked him straight in his own eye, with intention, ready to speak to him without malice. He saw God, the Butcher Father, who saw him in return.

"When she comes, follow her. She will show you the way."

The voice coming from the eye was reassuring.

"My son, I was wrong. Women aren't our enemy. Rose, their leader, is the Amazon, the way."

Charles looked at the eye in the pussy swallowed and spit out by its movement. He stared at the eye that was staring at him and time passed, nothing needed to be rushed. He was feeling good, he was waiting.

OLIVIER, BERTRAND, AND ANDRÉ ARRIVED. They were welcomed with champagne and Julie at the height of her gaiety, and by Rose, half naked, whose beauty and simpering airs threw André into a tizzy, since he was seeing her for the first time, and irritated Bertrand, who was also seeing her for the first time, so to speak, since she'd never acted this way around him. Rose was beginning a new career and testing her talents on them, at least that's what she told herself as she snorted a generous line of cocaine offered by André.

"Some wake-up, Bella."

Rose would fuck him, this Great Skirt-Chaser, tall, dark, and handsome, fuck him like use him, use him then throw him away afterwards, that's what she promised herself, but first she had to play out her plans.

Large white clouds travelled through the sky, and behind them the sun erupted here and there, like a spotlight aiming at them, scanning them and the city with its powerful burning.

Supercharged with cocaine, Julie was knocking on every door in the building to invite her neighbours up on the roof. "The more, the merrier!" she told every one of them, reassuring them afterwards, her words tumbling out, words juxtaposed—merry had nothing to do with Christmas, it was summer after all, and they just wanted to be happy, so they were welcome upstairs with their alcohol to contribute to the merriness. She knocked on Charles' door and got no answer, but she didn't worry herself too much. Before going down the hall in her flip-flops, she yelled through the door:

"Hey, Photoman! We're waiting for you! Hurry up!"

No sound came from behind the door. Too bad for him.

Olivier Blanchette tracked her with his camera, he'd decided that improvisation would be the rule of the shoot, chaos might be used later, in a manner yet to be determined.

Julie's rampage through the hall achieved its results. Two dozen bored neighbours accepted the invitation, they appeared one after the other on the roof, calling their friends on their cellphones, sensing electricity in the air, the promise of action. They decided to move the tables along the deck. The guardrail pitched a little, but that was no problem since everyone had been informed, in any case it had been collectively decided that if you were going to fall, you'd have to want to.

ROSE WAS STANDING in front of Charles who was watching her, his eyes bulging, his mouth half-open, like a child in front of a magician. Like Charles, Rose was exalted and more convinced than ever, his reaction was better than in her wildest dreams. She'd raised her turquoise dress over her hips with both hands, the white satin string shone in the dim room, a phosphorescent presence that spoke to Charles, showing him the way to go, with the voice of the Butcher Father commenting on every move, approving. In the darkness, the computer screen displayed Rose's pussy, and she could see the image. He's jerking off in secret instead of coming to me, she thought, happy at the prospect.

"I was waiting for you," Charles said.

"You want to turn on a light?" she asked.

And then, at the same time, "Turn on the light. Do what she asks," the Butcher commanded.

Charles turned on a light near them, then kneeled down in front of Rose, as if in prayer.

"Go ahead, I'm ready," he said.

"This is for you. I did it for you. A gift." Rose answered, her voice trembling.

"I know. I know," he whispered, bowing his head in respect.

Rose removed her string with the deliberate slowness of a striptease, and gently placed it on Charles' desk, then bent backward, still standing, her legs spread, her fingers opening her inner lips that had been shrunk, disappeared, her clitoris already swollen, enormous without its hood. Eyes closed, she awaited his touch, a sound, animal excitement, but nothing happened. Maybe he already came, she thought. It was a possibility.

After a minute without movement or hard breathing, she stood straight again and opened her eyes to see Charles still in prayerful attitude, staring at her pussy with his mouth open, maddened and serious. Against all expectations, his pants were still buttoned up and he wasn't touching himself, his hands lay against his legs, well-behaved.

"Look and see," the Father spoke. "It is the holy pussy that leads to the beyond."

Charles gazed upon her pussy, almost healed, waxed and offered up to him, he was losing himself in that little girl's vulva, in the middle of it there was an eye, the same as on the screen. Then, slowly, the movement of the worms took over Rose's flesh where the eye scanned left and right.

"Thank you, Rose, thank you. I didn't know. I was blind."

"What's up with you? What are you doing?" she yelled, forcing Charles to retreat, then look away from her pussy and at her face.

Rose was hurt, she had no idea what to do. She bent down and grabbed Charles' right hand and steered it between her legs.

"No!"

"What's wrong? What's happened to you?"

"It is forbidden! It is holy!"

Charles would not give her what she wanted. Rose understood. Brusquely, she pushed her dress back down and picked up her string. She waved it in Charles' face. He was terrified as he kneeled before this Last Judgement.

"Do you see these panties? This satin string? Do you see it? Huh? I bought it for you! For you!"

Rose shook the string violently and pointed at her crotch.

"Did you see the operation? Of course you did! It's for you too! I thought of you the whole time! Do you know what that means! No! You can't understand!"

She was on the edge of tears, and they were tears of rage.

"You don't even want to touch me! After everything I've done, you won't even bother touching me, Mister Clean!"

The voice of the Butcher, aggressive now, had turned into a woman's voice through Rose's anger. The voice seemed to come from Rose as if she had lost all material presence, but that non-presence was heading for the door.

"What are you waiting for? Touch her! Touch her!"

Charles got up and ran with outstretched arms toward Rose, who was moving through the doorway into the corridor, reaching the staircase, taking the stairs two at a time. Charles was at the mercy of the voice that hit high-pitched tones, and when he listened, it was his mother's voice, yes, it was Diane's voice that had joined in on some inexplicably logical plane, threatening him now.

"What have you done? You didn't listen to her! You didn't follow her! You're going to pay!"

Charles kneeled down and covered his ears with his hands to shut out the voices, but they continued unabated to threaten him. Then, other voices, known and unknown, superimposed themselves over Diane's, a dozen at least, a cacophony of imprecations, birds of ill omen.

"No! I'm sorry! I'll do anything she wants me to. Anything!"

But Charles could not get to his feet, he was crying, moaning, he was cold. Having sane thoughts was impossible now because They'd stolen them, and They'd replaced them with the Will. Turning toward his computer, he discovered it had switched to screen saver, and it was showing patterns upon patterns that were messages to decipher, all indicating the same direction: the roof.

ON THE ROOF there had to be fifty people, neighbours from the building and their friends, and the friends of their friends. "The more, the merrier!" Julie exclaimed, full of energy, repeating it until people started getting tired of her.

Rose appeared on the roof with promises of vengeance. Never had she felt so humiliated. She'd sacrificed herself for Charles in vain, and found herself with nothing at all. She walked through the crowd on the roof and everyone noticed her, so pretty and provocative with her too-short dress, balancing on her platform shoes, drinking champagne and muttering to herself, as André trailed her and tried to drag her into a corner of the deck, away from onlookers behind the stairwell, to offer her some cocaine and, while he was at it, to touch that small body engineered for fucking. Olivier Blanchette was alternating between Rose who was a spectacle in herself, and Julie voicing her opinions on the world that quickly turned to digressions.

Like Rose, Julie stalked through the crowd, the queen of the roof, making sure everyone had enough of everything, that they were all drinking their fill. She'd made herself up and done her hair in a hurry down in her apartment, and put on shorts and high-heeled shoes—why let Rose be the centre of attention?—and Bertrand was again trying to seduce her, again without success. The Hawaiian shirts he insisted on wearing, she didn't know why, they were the enemy of seduction, maybe because the pattern made her think of her grandfather O'Brien who spent every winter in Florida for the past twenty years. She was jabbering in all directions at once, telling everyone about the virtues of sunscreen and proper hydration, talking about her project to whomever would listen, and the shoot, and Charles the photographer who still hadn't made his way up to the roof but would soon, she was about to go get him. Almost all the sandwiches and salads left in the shade on a picnic table had been eaten, the guests were leaving the deck and coming back with more water, fruit juice, wine, and hard liquor, cases of beer, bags of ice, and bites to eat. Music too, techno and other genres, less popular, which Julie didn't know and didn't hear either, too caught up in her own words that she couldn't control.

"Where's Charles?"

Her eyes on Julie, Rose blew cigarette smoke over her head, an act of bravado, as if she didn't care.

"I don't know. Probably fighting it out with his screen, I guess."

Julie accepted Rose's acerbic comments as the price to pay so that her own debt to the other woman might be annulled, though Rose getting kicked onto the street hadn't done much for either Charles or herself.

"Speak of the devil," Rose said, raising her chin in Charles' direction. He had just appeared on the rooftop deck, his eyes fidgeting and fearful.

"Charles!"

Julie moved toward Charles as Rose fled in André's direction. André hadn't taken his eyes off her for a moment, since he was taller than everyone else by a good head, he could do just that.

"Is everything ok? What are the pictures like? I hope they're good, especially the ones of Rose! You didn't have trouble transferring them, at least? We're having a party here with the neighbours! You can see for yourself, right?"

Charles was tracking Rose, and not listening to Julie at all. Julie set herself directly in front of him, trying to make him look at her, an intentional harassment, an obstruction, a buzzing fly, a wasp. He was fearful, hard and cold, like someone whose life is in danger. Everything about him was on the razor's edge, tense, his eyes alighting on every guest, every object, jumping from one to the other without concentrating on any of them, as if looking for the emergency exit. He just realized that the deck was full of people, everything was moving, the sky was shifting, releasing its clouds like a smokestack, and those same clouds were falling back onto the roof and him; he was trapped in the this world transformed, saturated, ready to explode, the opposite of the void; hellish plenitude, a world that contained too much; he could feel that this overflow was causing the voices in him to explode in whistles, jeers, and sarcasm. What had happened? "They're here for Rose too," the voices brayed. "Rose," Diane repeated, "this is her vengeance, you loser!"

Images, pictures, voices, sky and cloud, people moving, everything turned into a single slab of matter, indefinable, with no clear limits. The distance between beings had disappeared. Skin like the surface of things had disappeared. Charles was pouring himself out, he spat himself out, excavated, the outside poured into him in the same movement that destroyed the limits of the world.

"Charles, answer me. What's wrong? I can tell something's wrong. Is it the pictures? You got other pictures that bothered you?"

"No, no. I'm okay. I need to speak to Rose."

Charles was having trouble distinguishing his voice from the others, he tried to pull away from Julie but she held him by the arm, and the gesture angered him.

"Stay," she said, lowering her voice, feeling she should be kind to him. "Stay a little and talk with me."

"I had to do something and I didn't do it. I have to do it now."

"Calm down. Calm down. Tell me about it, come here. Rose won't go anywhere, she'll wait for you."

It was true. Rose was here to stay, she wouldn't leave, she would give him the sign, not the other way around, he heard it in his head, through the mouths of the voices that kept him informed. Julie and Charles moved away from the crowd and sat under a parasol, one facing the other. He's gone insane, Julie understood. Then she remembered the guardrail.

"Listen to me carefully. I'm going to tell you something very important. The guardrail over there was struck by lightning and not repaired very well," Julie said, pointing. "Don't go near it, understood?"

"Understood."

"The guardrail! The guardrail! Struck by lightning! The guardrail!" shouted the voices that started repeating everything they'd heard.

"Stay here, I'll be right back. Don't move."

Julie went over to Rose, who was talking to André, the Great Skirt-Chaser. Rose was preoccupied by something she didn't want to share.

"Something's wrong with Charles. We have to keep an eye on him. I think he's going insane."

André heard it all and backed away out of politeness.

"Don't give a shit," Rose spat out.

Rose was having problems of her own. Julie understood that having problems was a real obsession for people in her life and it was a shame, she'd hadn't had this much fun in years. Then, like an old blanket thrown over her, the day's humidity began to crush her and dirty her, sudden fatigue took over, a weight to bear, the weight of the world was everywhere upon her, it added to the great weariness in her ideas that refused to take shape and fell into obsolescence even before they had time to form. Cocaine, that liar, was fading away, fleeing out the back door, like a thief into the night, her good mood in its bag, escaping with the energy it had given her, better to snatch it away.

Julie watched Charles for a few minutes to try to gauge his condition. He held himself apart from the crowd, still sitting, but seemed calmer, at most he looked like a man struggling with himself—but who wasn't these days? Whatever, no matter, she could try to help him tomorrow or the next day, after all, what would it change, it wouldn't be too late, and now Bertrand was walking toward him. He would be in good hands.

Julie ran downstairs to her place to touch herself up, did a line, looked at herself in the mirror, then went back to the roof, only to see Olivier Blanchette aiming his camera at Rose, lying on a picnic table like a woman on the beach, a towel underneath her, her legs crossed at the ankles, her shoes still on, enormous sunglasses on her nose which covered half her face. Next to Rose, she saw him, the man she wasn't expecting, she couldn't understand why he was here, but he was, talking with one of the tenants: Steve Grondin.

"Listen one, listen all!" Rose announced loudly when she saw Julie back on the roof. "Come see the star of Julie O'Brien's documentary in action! Witness the destiny of the Vulva-Woman! Admire and praise her!"

For the first time in her life, Rose was causing a scandal, and she had an audience for it. She had never felt so sure of herself, she would finally do something, the first in a series, she hoped, that would seal her existence through images that would soon travel the world via the Internet.

"Olivier, come a little closer! All of you, come closer!"

Julie moved nearer to Rose but didn't look at her. She didn't understand a thing; she had left her body and was watching Steve glancing around but not seeing her, as Charles distanced himself from Rose, he knew by instinct that he had to protect himself from the sight. Things weren't going according to divine plan, it was his fault, he was being punished.

"You too, Charles! Come closer and see the spot where men like you push women like me! And you too, Julie, come and judge with your own eyes this new burqa, fresh from the operating table! Come witness the results, they'll blow you away!"

On the roof everyone stopped talking and turned to Rose, with questioning eyes they looked at one another as Julie was caught in a nightmare: everything she'd worked so hard to forget was returning, and suddenly, the man through whom she had encountered death stood before her, and after all this time, she was forced out of herself, and cast into the shadows.

A few people began moving toward Rose, creating a movement that led to the entire crowd gathering around her, closing in, each convincing his neighbour that this was part of the shoot, a making-of for a documentary, a staged scene they were all invited to participate in, as if this was a game and they were the walk-ons. Olivier was still aiming his camera at Rose, who was stroking one of her legs with her fingertips, from her ankle to her groin, from her groin to her ankle, pushing up her dress by a centimetre each time, revealing her white satin G-string.

"Come, Julie! Come, Charles! It's our job to throw ourselves in other people's faces, isn't it?"

Charles heard Rose but didn't understand the meaning of her words, or the only meaning he could understand was his own rejection: Rose, who was the Way, the leader of the Amazons, was pushing him out of her project. He had failed, she was going to show her eye, that thing beyond everyone, when only he was meant to have access to it. His whole life he would have to live with one foot in the old world and the other in the new, the fabulous one, and he would be at home in neither. The voice of the Father, not aggressive now, but infinitely disappointed, pronounced his sentence:

"She was there, and you missed it."

Then came Diane's voice: "Now someone else will become the messenger."

Everyone was looking at Rose except Julie who had moved away from the circle, and Charles too, who knew he was lost and wandered toward the edge of the deck. He laid his hand against the split guardrail Julie had warned him about, the spot where it had been struck by lightning. "The guardrail! Destroyed by lightning! The guardrail! The place to go!" Many voices repeated in one voice. Rose was the centre of attention for fifty people, their backs to Charles who could see only their backs, who knew that on the other side were faces looking at Rose. They would see what he had, what had been prepared for him and that he could not take.

Then a sound rose up from the small crowd around Rose, a murmur, a mix of stupor and consternation, like a wave, overseen by the changing sky as a wind blew up to sweep away everything and mix together the elements of the world that continued to collide, a perpetual circular movement.

The cloud formations gained speed, white and grey forms nearing the deck like small snakes, their heads pointing to the ground, to Charles who believed they were coming for him, the sky lowering to surround him, and help him in his gentle fall. The voices weren't yelling or insulting him, the danger was now past, everything was over, the voices murmured with the crowd, the voices were surprised to see what the crowd was seeing, and the voice of the Father spoke for Rose as well: "That's good, that's good, that's very good." Charles watched the clouds descend upon him; he could see the sky at high tide washing him out, the noise of the crowd and the voices in the clouds were taking Charles, the voices were beckoning him, offering their hand— the time had come to take the road open to him, he could certainly not miss the opportunity a second time.

The guardrail gave way under the weight of his hand, he let himself fall without a sound, without resistance, he let himself fall the way you let yourself sink in the waters of a lake, with no effort, his body falling backwards, his face still turned to the clouds enshrouding him, facing the crowd with their backs to him, not looking at him, troubled, concerned, disturbed by Rose's pussy like a miracle, or an object of shame, insanity, but something strong and captivating in every possible meaning, the crowd couldn't keep from gazing at this pussy offered up to them, which sent out its song that Charles thought he could hear as he fell, followed by other voices that filled the space of the sky, praying for him, his father's voice as he took him under his wing when his body hit the ground.

On Colonial Avenue there was no one around, the street was empty, on the roof the crowd was breaking up, hesitating, some wanted to leave, others to stay. Everyone was stunned. Julie had found refuge on the far side of the deck, her eyes on the horizon, toward Jacques Cartier Bridge. Rose hadn't thought of what to do afterwards, it was such a shame to look so confused after committing such an act, after the epic moment. Olivier had stopped filming, he didn't know what to think, nor did André the Great Skirt-Chaser, or Bertrand who just wanted to cry. No one in the thinning crowd had noticed the guardrail that wasn't much different than what it had been before Rose's performance, no one wondered where Charles the photographer had gone, not even Julie who still hadn't gotten over Steve being there, even if he'd gone. The party was over.

A woman walking down Mount Royal Avenue saw the body land, and for a moment it made no sense to her; bodies falling from the heavens don't exist. She went toward it to witness the destruction. Charles' body was bent at impossible angles, both arms on the same side, one leg longer than the other and turned the wrong way. She moved away carefully and fearfully, on tiptoe, her eyes on the sky, digging through her handbag to find her cell phone.

In the cloudy sky, the movement was intensifying, the wind rattled the parasols on the roof, it was a warm wind that foreshadowed a storm. Montreal was just waking up to summer, and the festivities that would bring people into the streets, its beating heart, all the way till October.

THE END.

ABOUT THE AUTHOR

Nelly Arcan was born in the Eastern Townships of Quebec. Her first novel *Putain* (2001); English: *Whore* (2004), drawing on her experience working in the sex trade in Montreal, caused a sensation and enjoyed immediate critical and media success. It was a finalist for both the Prix Médicis and the Prix Femina, two of France's most prestigious literary awards. Three more novels followed establishing her as a literary star in Quebec and France: *Folle* (2004); English: *Hysteric* (2014), also nominated for the Prix Femina, *À ciel ouvert* (2007); English: *Breakneck* (2015), and *L'enfant dans le miroir* (2007). *Paradis, clef en main*; English: *Exit* (2009), her fourth novel, was completed just days before she committed suicide in 2009 at the age of thirty-six. A collection of short cultural criticism, *Burqa de chair* (2011); English: *Burqa of Skin* (2014), was issued posthumously.

ABOUT THE TRANSLATOR

Born, bred and raised in Montreal, Jacob Homel has translated or collaborated in the translation of a number of works, including *Toqué: Creators of a Quebec Gastronomy*, *The Last Genêt* and *The Weariness of the Self*. In 2012, he won the J.I. Segal Translation Prize for his translation of *A Pinch of Time*. He shares his time between Montreal and Asia.